Savannah Spectator Blind Item

The *Savannah Spectator* has been scooped!
A little bird told us that television journalist
Jasmine Carmody is about to expose a cover-up
involving one of Savannah's premiere families! It
seems that the party-loving, bachelor co-founder
of a chain of popular coffeehouses has had a
secret love child tucked away for the past three
years. No word on how this news will affect his
wealthy uncle's senatorial bid....

And just who is the child's mother? Is she a
wanton one-night stand? A gold-digger looking
for her fifteen minutes? Or is she the one
that got away, the one our bachelor has
never gotten over—the one who will
convert our confirmed bachelor into
a husband and father at last?

Savannah's single ladies are
holding their breaths!

D0424196

Dear Reader,

Thanks so much for choosing Silhouette Desire—*the* destination for powerful, passionate and provocative love stories. Things start heating up this month with Katherine Garbera's *Sin City Wedding*, the next installment of our DYNASTIES: THE DANFORTHS series. An affair, a secret child, a quickie Las Vegas wedding…and that's just the beginning of this romantic tale.

Also this month we have the marvelous Dixie Browning with her steamy *Driven to Distraction*. Cathleen Galitz brings us another book in the TEXAS CATTLEMAN'S CLUB: THE STOLEN BABY series with *Pretending with the Playboy*. Susan Crosby's BEHIND CLOSED DOORS miniseries continues with the superhot *Private Indiscretions*. And Bronwyn Jameson takes us to Australia in *A Tempting Engagement*.

Finally, welcome the fabulous Roxanne St. Claire to the Silhouette Desire family. We're positive you'll enjoy *Like a Hurricane* and will be wanting the other McGrath brothers' stories. We'll be bringing them to you in the months to come as well as stories from Beverly Barton, Ann Major and *New York Times* bestselling author Lisa Jackson. So keep coming back for more from Silhouette Desire.

More passion to you!

Melissa Jeglinski

Melissa Jeglinski
Senior Editor
Silhouette Desire

Please address questions and book requests to:
Silhouette Reader Service
U.S.: 3010 Walden Ave., P.O. Box 1325, Buffalo, NY 14269
Canadian: P.O. Box 609, Fort Erie, Ont. L2A 5X3

SIN CITY
WEDDING

KATHERINE GARBERA

Silhouette®

Desire

Published by Silhouette Books

America's Publisher of Contemporary Romance

Special thanks and acknowledgment are given to Katherine Garbera for her contribution to the DYNASTIES: THE DANFORTHS series.

 SILHOUETTE BOOKS

ISBN 0-373-76567-3

SIN CITY WEDDING

Visit Silhouette at www.eHarlequin.com

Printed in U.S.A.

Books by Katherine Garbera

Silhouette Desire

KATHERINE GARBERA

has had fun working as a production page, lifeguard, secretary and VIP tour guide, but those occupations pale when compared to creating worlds where true love conquers all and wounded hearts are healed. Writing romance novels is the perfect job for her. She's always had a vivid imagination and believes strongly in happily-ever-after. She's married to the man she met in Walt Disney World's Fantasyland. They live in Central Florida with their two children. Readers can visit her on the Web at www.katherinegarbera.com.

DYNASTIES: THE DANFORTHS

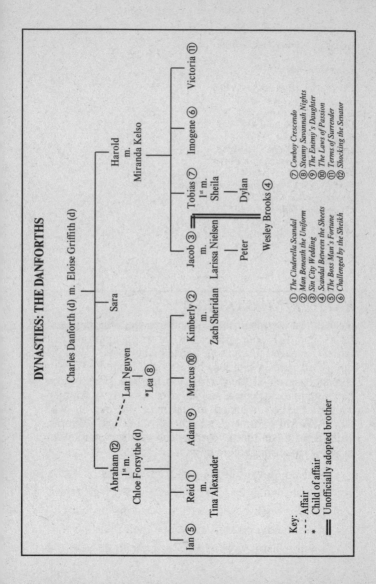

Charles Danforth (d) m. Eloise Griffith (d)

Abraham ⑫
1ˢᵗ m.
Chloe Forsythe (d)

Lan Nguyen
|
*Lea ⑧

Sara

Harold
m.
Miranda Kelso

Ian ⑤   Reid ①   Adam ⑨   Marcus ⑩   Kimberly ②
m.   m.
Tina Alexander   Zach Sheridan

Jacob ③   Tobias ⑦   Imogene ⑥   Victoria ⑪
m.   1ˢᵗ m.
Larissa Nielsen   Sheila

Peter   Wesley Brooks ④   Dylan

① The Cinderella Scandal
② Man Beneath the Uniform
③ Sin City Wedding
④ Scandal Between the Sheets
⑤ The Boss Man's Fortune
⑥ Challenged by the Sheikh

⑦ Cowboy Crescendo
⑧ Steamy Savannah Nights
⑨ The Enemy's Daughter
⑩ The Laws of Passion
⑪ Terms of Surrender
⑫ Shocking the Senator

Key:
- - - Affair
* Child of affair
══ Unofficially adopted brother

One

Larissa Nielsen had imagined how she'd look when she saw Jacob Danforth again. None of her ideas involved wearing her oldest pair of leggings and a tie-dyed Florida T-shirt. But the early-morning call from Jasmine Carmody, a reporter with the *Savannah Morning News*, had left Larissa no choice. She needed to talk to Jake before Jasmine told the world who Peter's father was.

Now Larissa was sitting in her car in front of Jake's Savannah town house like some crazy ex-girlfriend stalker. She wished she were just waking up back at her house in Riverside. She wished their morning routine wasn't disrupted and she and her three-year-old son could welcome the day on their dock overlooking the Savannah River. Instead, she was about to do something, her conscience reminded her, she should have done a long time ago.

She shone the light of her tiny flashlight on the pages in front of her. A collection of Robert Frost poetry had always been her saving grace. She'd used it to escape from life more than once and this morning, while she waited for time to creep by, it provided the escape she desperately needed from her chaotic thoughts.

A rap on the car window startled her. She glanced up to see the faint outline of a man. The man leaned down and she looked into dark brown eyes she'd never forgotten. His tough-guy look faded, replaced by a welcoming smile when he recognized her. She unlocked her door and Jake opened it.

Larissa wasn't a person anyone would call timid. But suddenly she felt like the Cowardly Lion. And it wasn't anything like the green floating head of the Great and Powerful Oz that scared her. She knew the man behind the curtain and she knew he would be royally pissed when she told him he had a three-year-old son.

Peter slept quietly in his car seat and she double-checked that his favorite blanket was tucked next to his chin before getting out of the car. The March morning air was chilly. She shivered a little and rubbed her hands on her arms, praying the tinted windows wouldn't reveal her son until she had a chance to tell Jacob herself.

"What are you doing parked in front of my house at seven in the morning?"

Jake was dressed in running shorts and a sleeveless T-shirt that was stained with sweat. He must have left before she'd arrived. She smoothed her hair down, wishing she'd had the time to make herself look more presentable.

He looked as good as she remembered. Would he feel as good? Somehow she knew he would, despite the fact that it had been almost four years since she'd had sex. She forced her gaze from his muscled chest to his face.

"It's a long story."

"About four years long?"

"You have no idea."

"Well, then let's get comfortable. Come inside and I'll make you some coffee. You know I'm famous for it."

She couldn't help but smile. Even when they'd been nothing more than friends, Jake had always been able to make her laugh. But she couldn't leave Peter sleeping in the car.

"Actually, I have something to tell you."

"And you can't do it inside?"

"Well…no."

She leaned back against the driver's door and tried to find the right words. She swallowed once then licked her lips. "Um…this is harder than I thought it would be."

"I wish I could help you out, Larissa, but I have no idea what you're trying to say."

She shook herself. She'd be matter-of-fact. She was known for her practicality. "Remember that night at the reunion."

"How could I forget?" he asked, running the tip of one finger down the side of her face. Shivers of awareness coursed through her. Jake had always elicited a response from her even when he wasn't trying to.

"I haven't forgotten it either," she said.

"Is that why you are here?" he asked. He leaned closer toward her, surrounding her with the heat of his body and his earthy scent. His dark eyes focused on her lips and she felt them tingle. Without thinking, she licked her bottom lip and he tracked the motions with his gaze. Dammit, this was getting out of hand. His touch on her face moved to her mouth, stroking her bottom lip with his thumb.

"Larissa Nielsen on my doorstep. I can't quite figure out why. Why now? Why are you here, Larissa?"

"A reporter contacted me about your uncle's senate bid." Larissa knew the only way to the truth was through the story of what had happened. Because the reason she'd been keeping Peter a secret hadn't changed and if Jasmine Carmody hadn't called her, Larissa would still be at home in Riverside watching the sun rise and drinking D&D Coffee's special morning blend.

"Those damned reporters. They won't leave any of us alone." Jake ran his fingers through his thick curly hair in a gesture she'd seen her son make when he was on the verge of a meltdown.

"I'm sorry," she said, knowing Jake treasured his privacy above just about anything else.

"Hey, babe, it's not your fault. So why are you here?"

"She knows about our one-night stand," Larissa blurted out.

"I wish you wouldn't call it that. I wanted to see you again."

He'd called her several times, but she'd dodged his calls. Eventually she'd moved to Atlanta with her college roommate to make sure Jake never found out their one night had consequences.

Jake hadn't been ready for fatherhood then. D&D's, the coffeehouse Jake had co-founded with his cousin Adam, had been about to go national and Jake hadn't really changed all that much since college. He was still the fun-loving, Saturday-morning-soccer-playing guy he'd always been. And she knew from bitter experience that a woman who tied a man down became a burden. She'd vowed long ago to never become a burden.

"I had my reasons for not meeting you in Cancun." She nibbled her lower lip. *Just tell him.*

"Our one night together isn't really that newsworthy, honey. Don't worry about that."

"Actually, it is," Larissa said.

"Why, did the reporter have pictures?" Jake asked with a bad-boy grin that brought that night back in vivid detail. It had been a steamy summer night, and in his arms she'd felt like the most beautiful woman in the world, not the plain Jane she'd always been.

"Yes, but not of us."

"Then who?" he asked, becoming exasperated.

Oh, God. "Our son."

Jake staggered back from her. "Did you say son?"

"Yes, his name is Peter, Peter Jacob, and he's three years old."

Jacob reached for the back door but it was still locked. "Unlock it."

She did and he opened the door and looked down on their sleeping son. Peter's curly hair was the same dark shade as Jake's. He reached out for Peter's head with a touch so gentle that she knew she'd made a mistake in not telling him sooner.

But the past had taught her a bitter lesson, and she'd always dreamed that her life would be sit-com perfect. Instead reality was very different. All the excuses she'd made to herself for the past three years sounded lame now and when Jake glanced up at her, she knew he'd think so, too.

"My son," he said, looking down on Peter with a wealth of emotions that she hadn't suspected Jake could feel.

* * *

His son. He still couldn't really take it in. Parenthood was an alien concept to Jake. He reached for the buckle on the car seat but couldn't figure out how to operate it. Nothing in his life had prepared him for this. He'd have to give his brother Toby a call later; he was the only expert on fatherhood he knew.

''Get him out,'' he said to Larissa. His hands were shaking. He was a father.

She brushed past him. Her slender body had remained unchanged over the years since they first met. Her clear blue eyes had always struck him as the most honest he'd ever looked into—until today.

Larissa put her hand on his back and leaned into the car. One of her breasts brushed against his side and arousal moved through him like lightning. He felt the heat from her hand on the small of his back burn through his shirt.

She pushed against him as she leaned into the car, balancing herself with the touch on his back. Reaching out, she ruffled Peter's hair. ''Morning, sleepyhead.''

''Morning, Mama,'' he said.

They had a bond. A bond that Jake had never wanted but now suddenly envied. Maybe this was what he'd been searching for lately. Maybe this would fill the restlessness that his work and partying couldn't.

Jake reached for his son and the boy recoiled, pulling a ragged-looking bear and a tattered blanket closer. Tucking the edge of the blanket between his lips, Peter looked at Larissa.

"It's okay, baby. Jake's a friend." Larissa turned toward him, her breath brushing across his cheek. Her mouth was fuller than he'd remembered.

"He's kind of shy around new people," Larissa said.

"The word *Dad* is foreign to him?" Jake asked, to remind himself that Larissa wasn't the sweet girl from his memories. She was the woman who'd had his child and kept it a secret.

"He's only three. Some things take time to remember."

"Did you have a problem remembering too?" he asked sarcastically.

Jake had always loved women. He'd never had any trouble with them. Women were meant to be protected, he knew, even though his track record on this front wasn't great. But how did you protect someone who had betrayed you?

She sighed. "If you're going to treat me the way I deserve to be treated, I'm going to take Peter home and come back by myself. To him you're a stranger who's mad at his mom."

He realized she was right. For better or worse, Peter's entire world revolved around Larissa. And making Larissa cry or angry probably wouldn't help Peter to like him. He straightened from the car and took the two steps back to the sidewalk.

She lifted their son out, brushing a soft kiss against the top of his head and rubbing his back before setting the boy on the sidewalk. It was obvious how deeply Larissa cared for her son. He shouldn't be surprised. She'd always had a nurturing quality about her. Originally it was what had drawn him to her.

Peter clung to the back of Larissa's leg, watching Jake with the same intensity that his mother did. Why hadn't she trusted him enough to tell him he had a son?

"Did that reporter follow you?" he asked.

"I don't think so."

"Let's go inside just to be safe."

She nodded and bent to pry her son's hands from her thigh. She took the small hand in her own and as Jake watched them, he realized the two of them were watching him. Waiting to see what he'd do. Frankly, he was out of his element.

He bent down on one knee and held out his hand to his son. Peter hesitated, then handed Jake the bear. "Oh, he's giving you Mr. Bear. That means he likes you."

"I'm glad one of you does," Jake said.

Larissa watched him with those soulful eyes of hers. And he felt like a big mean bully. He tried to get past his anger so he could remember all the reasons he liked her but he couldn't.

"Oh, Jake this isn't about liking you," she said, softly.

He glanced up at her. "Then what is it about?"

"Me not being the right woman for you."

"Well, I do tend to like a different sort of woman."

"I know. Tall, blond and built."

"Nice opinion you've got of me, Rissa. But I'm not that shallow. I meant honest. I like my women to be honest."

She flushed. He knew that anything else he said now would be mean and sarcastic, but sending her away with the son he'd just discovered wasn't an option.

He pivoted on his heel without saying another word. Unlocking the door to his town house, he turned left and entered his living quarters. The living room was sleek and sophisticated. All chrome, glass and Italian leather. The entertainment center was top of the line and he'd just had a new large-screen plasma TV installed on Friday.

Larissa and Peter stood in the doorway as if afraid to enter. How old was his son? He knew she'd told him, but he'd been trying to grapple with the fact that he was a father and hadn't paid attention. It had been almost four years since he'd seen Larissa so Peter would have to be about three. What did kids that age do?

"Does he watch TV?"

"Yes. But only PBS."

Figures, Larissa would be all about educational television. He looked at the serious little boy.

His son. He felt a stirring so deep inside that it made his anger pale. This was his son. His future was tied to this little boy, and he knew he had to make the situation right.

He knelt in front of Peter again. The boy had his eyes. He studied Peter until the boy reached out and touched the stubble on his chin. "You're prickly."

"I didn't have time to shave yet."

Peter glanced up at Larissa. "How come you don't feel like that?"

"Girls don't," she said.

"Girls are different," Peter said, turning back to Jake.

"They sure are."

"You got any food?" Peter asked.

"Peter."

"It's okay. Come on, I'll fix us some breakfast." He stood and led Peter down the hall to the kitchen. "Then your mom and I need to talk."

Jake seated Peter at the large butcher-block table and checked the pantry for something a little boy might want to eat. He had two jars of martini olives and a box of water crackers. The fridge held several bottles of wine, a six-pack of Coors and an opened bottle of champagne. Maybe Wes had eggs in his fridge. His best friend lived upstairs.

"I probably should have found a sitter for Peter," Larissa said.

He turned to look at her. Peter was occupied at the table with an electronic book that Larissa must have had in that big purse of hers.

"I'm glad you didn't," he said.

She was so close he could smell the fragrance of her shampoo. She wore no makeup. But then she rarely did. Her skin was smooth and fine, creamy looking. Lust surged inside him, which further enraged him. He didn't want to want her.

She swallowed and he knew that she still wasn't sure letting him know his son was a good idea. He wondered how much of it stemmed from his reputation and how much of it came from her knowledge of him.

He'd never really taken responsibility seriously. Everyone in the family knew it. And thanks to the media coverage of his uncle's senate bid, most of the public knew it too. He was the fun-loving, thirty-year-old millionaire with the Midas touch. But Larissa should know better, especially when she'd found out she was having his son.

"What do you want to eat, sport?"

"Pancakes."

"Uh…let's see what I've got." Jake had no idea how to make pancakes. He could scramble eggs but there weren't any in the fridge. "I can run upstairs to see if Wes has some eggs."

"Your college roommate Wes?"

"Yeah, you remember him."

"Don't bother. Surely you have some cereal."

"Frosted Sugar Os and Captain Crunch."

"He'll have toast with butter."

"Educational TV and healthy food. Larissa, does our boy get to have any fun?"

"Of course, he does. Just not bad influences."

"Is that why you never called me?" he asked.

"What?"

"Am I a bad influence for our son?"

"No. Never."

She closed the distance between them, reaching up to touch him and then dropped her hands. "The reasons are complicated. Let's get Peter settled, then we can talk."

He nodded. He'd wanted her to touch him. Needed her to in a way that made him feel vulnerable, reminding him that he was just a man and had more weaknesses than he wanted to acknowledge.

The toast was buttered and eaten in short order. Jake grabbed a soccer ball from the closet, and now that the morning sun was shining brightly, they took it outside. Peter kicked the ball, chasing it from one end of the yard to the other.

He gestured for Larissa to sit down on the chaise and dragged over one of the Adirondack chairs he'd made last summer.

He watched his son running after the ball on pudgy legs. Larissa had taken something from him that he could never get back. Though deep inside he allowed he probably wouldn't have been ready for fatherhood three years ago, he still felt betrayed.

Jake suddenly thought of his father. God, the old man was going to be extremely disappointed when Jake told him he had a three-year-old son. Just one more screwup from a son who never measured up.

Larissa sat there looking much the same as she had in their college days. A sweet innocent who didn't really fit in at Georgia Tech. He'd befriended her because she'd reminded him of his younger sisters and he would've wanted Victoria and Imogene to have found a guy who'd do the same.

But all of that faded when he glanced at their little boy. "I'm so angry I want to shake you."

TWO

Larissa had been hoping that Jake would just jump on the problem with the reporter, but she should've known better. He was a detail man who liked to get all his facts in order before making a decision. Many times during their college days, he'd used her as a sounding board for his theories and ideas before drawing a conclusion. She leaned back in the lounge chair and took a sip of her coffee.

"Stalling is not going to make me less angry," he said.

"I know." She watched her small son chasing the ball across the yard and tried to find the words to tell Jake that she'd kept Peter a secret for herself and for him. She hadn't wanted Peter to grow up in a household similar to the one she had.

Her parents had married because her mother had been pregnant. From her earliest memories Larissa was aware that if she hadn't been born, her parents wouldn't have been married. Theirs was an unhappy house. So she sought refuge in a world of books, creating her dreams from the stories she cherished. Tales of epic love and vanquishing heroes.

But the real world wasn't full of those epic love stories she'd dreamed of for her life. And instead of being a fair lady waiting in her tower to be rescued, Larissa's fate had become her mother's.

"I'm waiting," Jake said, his voice quiet and deep with suppressed emotion. Her heart ached because she knew how hard it had always been for Jake to express his emotions. To the outside world he presented his devil-may-care bachelor image but Larissa knew that Jake's emotions ran deep. He was anything but carefree.

She studied Jake's face. He was so familiar to her, not just because of his resemblance to their son. But because she saw his face every night in her dreams. Even before Peter was born, Jake had been the one man she'd never been able to forget.

Perhaps it was because of their friendship. She'd survived her college years at Georgia Tech because of him. Unlike the other guys who'd looked right through her, Jake had seen her.

He'd been her first male friend. The first man she'd trusted. The only man she'd ever really been comfortable with.

She couldn't tell him that she'd kept their son a secret because she'd been afraid that one day he'd leave her for a more glamorous woman and perhaps take their son with him.

"Everything about Peter is complicated."

Jake sat on the edge of her lounge chair and touched her face carefully. She knew in that instant that however Jake saw her, it wasn't the way other men did. "It doesn't have to be. Just level with me."

When he touched her she couldn't think. Shivers of awareness spread throughout her body and she'd never been more aware of Jake's maleness.

The fact that he was filled with rage at the secret she'd kept for too long didn't make it any easier to stop her skin from tingling, her nipples from tightening, or the warmth from pooling between her legs. She closed her eyes. But that only intensified his touch. It brought the entire focus of her world down to the two of them and the warmth of his fingers on her face.

"I'm waiting, Rissa."

Rissa, Jake was the only person who'd ever cared enough to call her by a nickname. To the world she was the serious librarian who could find any fact in record time, but to Jake she'd always been...she wasn't sure what she'd been to him. Or what she would be now.

She opened her eyes and his face was barely an inch from hers. His breath brushed her cheek and she knew if she leaned the tiniest bit toward him, he'd take control of this unexpected embrace. His lips would touch hers and she'd give up reason and sanity to experience again the magic they'd shared on that long-ago night.

She cleared her throat and leaned away from him. He rubbed his fingers, which had just been touching her face, and looked at her with regret.

"I'm not sure where to begin. The reasons are long and complicated. And you're too angry to really listen."

"Any man would be."

"I'm not saying you shouldn't be. I just don't want to become a victim in your quest for vengeance."

He watched her for a moment then stood in a rush, cursing under his breath. She realized she was right.

She should have known better. She'd never been more than a rather average looking woman and Jake…well, Jake was used to prime cuts of womanhood. Tall, leggy blondes with D cups and flawless complexions. The closest she'd come to a D cup was after Peter had been born and her milk had come in.

"Then let's get this talk about our son over with."

She took a deep breath. She felt even more vulnerable than she had when she'd arrived at his house this morning. "I don't know what to say."

"For God's sake, woman, you graduated from Georgia Tech with honors. How hard can it be for you to find the words?"

"I wish it were easier, but it's all tied to my feelings."

"About me? I didn't force you that night."

"Jake, I was there, remember? It was an incredible night. I don't have any lingering resentment from that."

"I knew it."

"Good thing we're outside."

He quirked one eyebrow at her in question.

"So that your swelled head has room."

"Start from the beginning. I thought I used a condom."

"I think it broke."

"What?"

"I was a little sticky the next morning. So I took a test as soon as possible."

"You knew when I called to ask you to go to Cancun?"

"Yes."

Jake turned away from Larissa, intent on leaving before he said something he'd regret. Larissa was watching him with tears in her eyes and his head told him there was no way she'd intended to hurt him with her decision. But right now his heart told him he didn't care.

He felt betrayed because he'd always trusted Larissa. If any of the other women he'd slept with had shown up on his doorstep with a child in tow, he'd know they were there for money. He was always careful about protection because he knew that his name and his money left him vulnerable to ambitious women.

But Larissa was the sweet girl he'd felt comfortable talking to in the late hours at the library. The woman who'd come back to their five-year reunion looking like the embodiment of every female fantasy he'd ever had. The woman who'd come to him today for help whether she admitted it or not.

And he was in no mood to help. He had to shake the fury pumping through him with every beat of his heart.

"I'll be back," he said, and walked into his house.

He headed down the hall to his tae kwon do workout room. In the corner was a bag he used for kickboxing practice and for sparring when Wes wasn't available to work out. He closed off his thoughts. Centered himself and focused all of his energy on the punching bag. Twenty minutes later he was dripping with sweat and still not sure he was ready to talk to Larissa. But they didn't have the luxury of time. There was a reporter who was determined to flash his face across the front page of every paper with the word *father* in the headline. He had to step up to the plate. He had to drop the safety of his carefree existence and really make his life count.

He bit back a savage curse. He wasn't ready for this. Didn't know that he ever would be. But Peter—that little boy—and his family deserved better. His uncle had enough to worry about with his campaign and some vaguely threatening e-mails. Jake wasn't going to add Larissa and Peter to the mix.

Grabbing a monogrammed towel from the rack near the door, he walked through his house. His town house had been featured in *Modern Architecture* as the ultimate bachelor pad. He grabbed a bottle of water from the fridge before stepping out on his patio. He wasn't sure what he expected to find when he returned.

He knew it wasn't Larissa sitting on the grass with their son in her lap. Both of them had their eyes closed and faces turned to the sun. He thought they were sleeping but then realized that Larissa was speaking softly. The words were familiar to him. Robert Frost's poem *Stopping by Woods on a Snowy Evening*.

He'd never felt more inadequate for the task before him than he did at this moment. Sure, *Fortune* magazine had called him and Adam the golden boys of the coffee bean world, "taking a tried and true idea and making it new and fresh."

But fatherhood was different. It involved emotions

and all kinds of variables that didn't work in a solid business plan. And emotion was the one thing he'd always felt most uncomfortable with.

He guessed that was partly why he had a son with Larissa. The night of the reunion he'd realized she'd become more than just a smart girl who'd listen to him ramble on about what he wanted to do with his life. And he'd been uncomfortable with all she'd made him feel. Except for the passion she'd evoked in him. Passion was one area he was extremely comfortable with. So he'd seduced her under the stars.

Watching mother and child now kindled a desire for something that he hadn't realized was missing from his life. He wanted to be a part of that golden circle of light. Of that deep bond between mother and son. He wanted to insure that Rissa and Peter could always find a patch of sunlight to sit in. He set his towel and water bottle down on the table and crossed to them.

Not questioning his actions, he sank to the ground behind Larissa and settled himself around her. He left a couple of inches of space because he knew that in spite of his feelings of betrayal, he wasn't above using sex to manipulate her. He wanted her like hell on fire. And if he touched her again, he wasn't going to be able to control himself.

He put his hands over Larissa's and felt her stiffen. Peter's small hand moved to rest on his wrist and Jake felt something close to peace for the first time since he'd been old enough to know that he was a Danforth.

He liked the sound his deep voice made added to Larissa's soft tone and Peter's childish one.

"The woods are lovely, dark and deep
  But I have promises to keep
  And miles to go before I sleep
  And miles to go before I sleep."

They finished the poem together and Peter leaned around his mother to watch him with wide questioning eyes.

"How did you know the words?" Peter asked.

"Your mom taught them to me," he said, softly. The boy continued to watch him with a focus that was unnerving.

Peter broke into a wide grin and said, "Cool." The boy hopped to his feet and ran across the yard toward the ball.

Jake turned his head a quarter and met Larissa's clear blue gaze. For a moment they were back in the uncomplicated days of college. Life was just about doing what felt right and making each moment count. Victoria had still been safely at home, and he hadn't yet fathered a child. But times had changed and Victoria was gone—disappeared at a concert so long ago. And though everyone warned them she was dead and would never return, Jake's family kept hope alive.

Larissa smiled at him and his groin tingled. She

was so close that her scent filled his nostrils with each breath.

"I did, didn't I?" She licked her lips nervously and he leaned closer to her. Her mouth had always fascinated him. Her lower lip was fuller than the top and he knew from that one brief night how sumptuous her mouth would feel under his own.

He leaned farther toward her, but Peter used his wrist for balance as he stood and then raced across the yard to the soccer ball.

"Yes, you did," he said to Larissa.

"That seems like so long ago."

"It was a different life," he said.

Peter kicked the ball over to them with more energy than skill. Jake had always been very good at soccer and his son showed…none of Jake's aptitude.

"Where'd you go before?" Peter asked, coming over to them.

"To my workout room. I needed to clear my head."

"Is it clear now?"

"Almost," Jake said, ruffling his son's hair.

He stood and helped Larissa to her feet. He still wanted to know why she hadn't told him she was having his child, but he'd save that conversation for later when they were alone. Right now they needed to figure out what to do next.

But Peter was watching him and he didn't want to have an uncomfortable conversation in front of the boy. "Let me show you how to kick the ball like the pros do."

"What's a pro?" Peter asked.

"A professional player. You know someone who gets paid to play the game."

"You can get paid to play?" Peter asked.

"Only if you're really good."

Jake showed his son a few basic kicks and then got out his practice goal net and left his son playing.

Larissa had returned to her lounge chair and watched him warily as he walked toward her. He didn't like the look on her face. He didn't like it at all.

Larissa tried not to stare as Jake walked over to her, but she couldn't help it. Sweat glistened on his neck and she knew that if she got close to him, he would smell earthy. She wanted to indulge herself in him once more. But he needed answers and she'd come here this morning intent on giving them to him.

She closed her eyes. While Jake had been gone, she'd found the words she needed to tell him. She'd have to sacrifice her pride, but Peter was more important than pride.

Jake returned and sat on a chair facing her. He braced his elbows on his knees and leaned toward her. She took a deep breath.

"Jake, I—"

"Larissa, I—"

She laughed. In the old days when they'd been friends, often they'd both started talking at the same time.

"You first," Jake said.

Knowing that Jake had never been anything but good to her, she sorted out the pieces of her troubled past and took a deep breath. "The reason why I didn't tell you about Peter is that I wanted to manage parenthood on my own."

"You always were pretty stubborn about that. Why don't you save the rest of the tale for a time when we are alone? Let's talk about what we do now."

She appreciated the reprieve, but she was curious. "What made you change your mind?"

He shrugged massive shoulders. "Something about you looking at me like I was an ogre."

"I didn't."

"Sweetheart, you have the biggest, most innocent eyes I've ever looked into, and it only takes one instant for you to make me feel like a bully."

His words made her feel special. "I didn't mean to."

"I know. Let's fix this reporter problem and then we'll talk. We'll find a sitter for Peter and we can learn each other's secrets."

"I don't have any secrets."

"Peter's it?"

"Yes, just Peter. I felt so…panicked when Jasmine Carmody called and said she knew you were Peter's father. There's nothing I can do to protect him from anything she writes for her newspaper. At least he can't read.''

"How did she find out about Peter? Am I listed on the birth certificate?''

"No. She said she'd talked to Marti Freehold. Do you remember her?''

"She's the biggest gossip I've ever met.''

"Yes, she is. Marti mentioned she'd seen us leaving the reunion together. And that we'd looked, well, like we needed to find a private room and quick.''

"Sounds like Marti,'' Jake said.

"Jasmine Carmody has Peter's birth certificate and she knows you're not listed on there, but she also has a picture of you when you were the same age as Peter. They're practically identical.''

Jake leaned back in the chair and Larissa tried not to stare at him. She knew that he was trying to solve a very sticky problem. And she shouldn't be lusting over him at a time like this.

Finally he cleared his throat. "I think I may have come up with a solution that will take the sting out of any article Jasmine Carmody writes.''

"What?''

"We'll live together as a family.''

"Will that work?''

"Sure it will. What she's doing is just a step above blackmail. If we acknowledge it and move on, then she can't hurt us with whatever she writes. I think it's the perfect solution."

"But living together? I don't think that's necessary."

"I do. I want to get to know my son. We'll be a family unit and once she knows I've acknowledged Peter is mine, she won't be able to hurt us."

"Jake, we hardly know each other."

He raised his eyebrow at her. "I'd say we know each other pretty well."

"That was just one night."

"Rissa, I was talking about all those late-night conversations in the library."

She flushed, knowing good and well what he'd been referring to. She wasn't sure what had changed while Jake had been gone, but his workout had brought back the man she knew. The man she was comfortable with. The man who wasn't so angry at being left in the dark where his son was concerned.

"Still, we've never lived together. I mean, where would we live?"

"I don't have every detail planned. I'd like to live here because I'm close to D&D's and I go into the office every day when I'm not traveling."

"Well, your place isn't much farther than mine from the library. But I don't know that I'd feel comfortable in your house."

"We'll hire a decorator to do the place over."

"I don't know. That seems like a big expense for…"

"For what?"

"For camouflage."

"Camouflage?" he asked.

"We aren't in a relationship. Are you sure about this?"

"One-hundred percent certain."

"Would we be like roommates?"

"What did you have in mind?" he asked, waggling his eyebrows at her.

She didn't know if she could live with Jake and not give in to the lust surging through her. This was probably the dumbest idea ever but deep in her heart it felt right.

"Not what you're thinking. I mean we're both adults. We can keep our hands to ourselves. We're living together for Peter's sake, not for ours."

"It's precisely because we are adults that I think we're going to have a hard time living together and not sleeping together."

"Jake, are you trying to say I can break your will-power?"

"Sweetheart, do you really want to start a battle over this?"

"Why, don't you think I could win?"

"Not if I put my mind to it."

"It's not your mind that tempts me, Jake."

He threw his head back and laughed. Her heart

clenched and her entire body ached. She wanted to be in his arms again. But she knew better than anyone did what a relationship based on a child was like. She also knew that when it came to lasting relationships, the odds of her and Jake making it work were very slim.

Her only chance at sanity was to make sure he stayed out of her bed and her heart.

Three

Jake knew there was no way he'd be able to live under the same roof as Larissa and keep his hands to himself. But if she wanted to pretend a platonic relationship was all she wanted, he'd let her. Passion and proximity were two things that couldn't be ignored.

He'd been celibate for a while now. Though he still casually dated, sleeping with women he hardly knew had lost some of the excitement it had held. And his business took most of his time. Becoming a millionaire in his own right before he turned thirty had taken all of his concentration.

The spark that had been kindled at their college

reunion almost four years ago hadn't died after one night together. This morning had proved that the fire between them still burned strongly. But he was willing to bide his time until they had everything settled between them before he made any moves toward Larissa.

He knew that in time she'd be in his bed. Everything else about the future seemed uncertain, but there was a sense of rightness in his soul when he thought of the two of them together. Just to be certain that he never lost his son again, he made a mental note to call Marcus, his cousin and family lawyer.

"You can move in today. Do you need my help to get your stuff?"

Larissa got to her feet and paced around the patio. Peter was still playing by the soccer net Jake had set up. Larissa watched her son for a few minutes, then turned back to him. "Not today. Let me think about this."

Jake moved near to her. She crossed her arms over her chest and stepped back from him. What was she afraid of? "What's to think about? No sex and we'll live here."

She bit her lip. "For how long?"

Jake shrugged. His experience with relationships said that most didn't last longer than it took to get your stuff settled, but Peter guaranteed they'd be together longer. "I don't know. Why?"

"What if one of us falls in love with someone

else?'' Larissa asked. The wind caught a strand of her hair, which brushed across her face. Larissa reached up and tucked it behind her ear.

Love was the one thing he'd never really found with any woman. It seemed elusive to him somehow. He wondered sometimes if love and happiness were going to be forever out of his reach. He was jaded enough to know that he wasn't going to find love through the intense desire that he felt for Larissa. ''I doubt that would happen.''

''Why not?'' she asked, holding herself tighter while she waited for his answer.

He didn't like the barrier she'd built between them. Didn't like that she was comforting herself and that she was still hiding something from him. So he said the one thing sure to needle her. He remembered her soft heart and belief in happily-ever-after.

''Because love is part of the game that people play when they are searching for themselves. We're both secure in our place in the world.''

She fisted her hands and put them on her hips. ''That is the stupidest thing I've ever heard.''

This was the Larissa he remembered. Eyes shooting sparks when he pushed her buttons. She'd been so sure she was a plain Jane who no jock would ever look at twice. But she'd caught his eye and held it longer than any of her peers back then. ''Surely, you don't believe in love?''

"Of course I do. And I'm raising our son to believe in it, too," she said, gesturing to Peter.

"You're just preparing him for heartache."

"Is that what love means to you?" she asked. Despite her argument, he didn't think she believed in love, either. Because any woman who had a romantic look on life would have contacted her baby's father.

He didn't like the direction this conversation was taking. "I don't know what love means to me. I can honestly say I've never really experienced it. Have you?"

"No."

"I don't think we'll have a problem with either of us falling in love. You're down-to-earth and so am I."

"I don't want to be a burden to you, Jake. I don't want to wake up one morning and find out you don't want us anymore."

"Why would that happen? I don't have time for anything else right now. D&D's keeps me busy and I'm not dating anyone."

"Right now, but you change women as often as you change your pants."

"That's not true. I haven't been with a woman in the last year and a half."

"Sure, you haven't."

"Believe what you want but I've never lied to you."

"Low blow."

"The truth hurts."

"I don't think this will work. Maybe I should take Jake and leave Savannah."

"You can leave if you want to, but you're not taking my son." Jake wasn't going to waste a single day of his time with Peter now that he knew he had a son. His dad, who'd always been busy with the shipping company, had made time for family. He wanted the opportunity to do the same.

She rubbed her eyes with the heels of her hands and then looked at him. He knew this was hard on her and he sympathized with her to a certain extent but they wouldn't be in this predicament now if she'd come to him when she'd first found out she was pregnant. "I don't know what to do. But I don't want to make things worse than they are now."

"I'll take care of everything for you."

"I'm not looking for a hero."

"Good, because I'm not much of one," he said. He'd always known his own faults.

He wanted to reach out and touch her. To take her in his arms and promise he'd shoulder her burdens, but he knew she wouldn't accept that. "Trust me on this, Rissa. I'll take care of everything."

"You aren't doing this for revenge, are you?"

"I don't follow."

"You know, make me move in here and then…do something to keep Peter and kick me out?"

"That's a nice opinion you have of me."

"Well, I wouldn't blame you if you tried it."

"You're important to Peter," he said. Larissa was the center of Peter's world and his son was the most important person to consider.

"People are going to say I trapped you."

"Let them talk. Anyone who knows you won't believe it."

"It's easy for you to say."

"Nothing about this is easy for me."

"I know. So we'd live with you until your uncle's campaign is over? Then the media scrutiny around your family will die down and we can go back to our normal lives."

"I'm not going to disappear after this reporter moves on to her next juicy topic." He realized the words were true as he said them. Larissa and Peter were his responsibility now and forever. And whether she lived with him or not, he'd always be involved in their lives. And that felt right to him deep in his soul.

"Promise?" The word was hardly out before Larissa bit her lip wishing she could take it back.

Jake closed the gap between them and cupped her face in his big hands. His brown eyes more serious than she'd ever seen them before, he leaned close to her. There were hidden depths to this man she'd scarcely explored.

She wondered what he'd do if she turned the tables

on him—if she held his face in her hands and looked down on him with something like tenderness.

"I promise."

She shivered. This was the secret dream she'd harbored since she was a young girl. That she'd find a man, a big, strong, attractive man who'd make her feel that she was the center of his world. But her dream had always been a bittersweet one, because time and experience had taught her that being the center of any man's world was a fleeting thing.

"Oh, Jake, don't say things you don't mean."

"Woman, I don't know why you have such a low opinion of me."

"I don't. It's myself I don't trust."

"What's not to trust?"

"You. Saying things that I'll take to mean something you aren't feeling."

"This isn't the love thing again, is it?"

"Don't be flip."

"I can't help it. You make me want to be a better man than I know I can be."

She was flattered that he thought she had any power over him. And saddened to realize that Jake thought he wasn't a great man to begin with. "Really?"

"Really."

"There you go again, making me believe you could be my knight in shining armor," she said, feeling her control shatter.

"I thought we both agreed I was no hero."

"When you touch me I can't think of anything but you."

"Rissa," he said. Lowering his mouth to hers, he brushed his lips back and forth over her own. It was a simple, gentle kiss, but it shook the moorings of everything she believed about herself.

She brought her hands to his shoulders, holding on to him for balance in a world that was suddenly spinning further and further out of her control. He traced the shape of her mouth with his tongue, running it over the closed seam of her lips. She knew what he wanted—what they both wanted. She opened her mouth on a sigh. And he teased her with his tongue. Teased her by giving her a hint of what was yet to come.

She leaned into him, resting against his strong body. She felt safe and in danger at the same time. Her breasts were heavy and she threw back her shoulders, rubbing their tips against him. He moaned deep in his throat, the sound feral and arousing.

Sliding his hands down her neck and then around to her back, his hold on her changed. He traced the line of her spine with his fingertips and she shuddered. She felt him tremble, too.

Jake pulled her more firmly against his body. His groin nestled into the notch at her thighs, her legs turned to jelly. She sank against him, totally caught up in his embrace. Jake supported her completely with one hand on her backside and the other behind her neck.

She moaned deep in her throat, tunneling her fingers through his hair to try to control their embrace. Or to at least be an active participant in it. He rubbed his tongue over hers and then pulled back.

Watching her intently, she couldn't help but wonder why she'd stayed away so long. But she knew the answer—because sanity was hard to come by and Jake threatened hers. She pulled away, tripping over her own feet in her hurry to put some distance between them.

Jake steadied her with one hand. His touch was warm but not soothing against her arm. She wanted to say the heck with her reservations and just indulge herself in a red-hot affair with this man. But there were too many barriers between them. Not the least of which was a little boy who deserved a happier childhood than Larissa had experienced.

She'd promised herself to protect Peter. No matter what the cost to her. Peter hadn't asked to be born and it was up to her make sure he had the best life had to offer. And Jake, for all his playboy ways, seemed genuinely interested in being a father to his son.

She knew she couldn't keep Jake and Peter apart. She'd have to make sure that Peter never knew the circumstances that had brought Jake and her together.

If things didn't work out between her and Jake, she didn't want Peter to feel it was his fault.

"Are you sure about the platonic part of this relationship?" Jake asked.

"You're the one who suggested it," she said. More than ever, she thought. Her blood was racing through her body. Her nipples were beaded and aching for his touch. And her center was wet with desire for him. She wanted to take his hand and lead him into the house where they could be alone. Only the knowledge that her son was a few feet away kept her from taking such an ill-advised action.

"Rissa?" he asked, running his finger down the side of her face.

"Yes," she said. She had to get out of this place. Figure out what was going on in her life and make a plan to protect herself from the vulnerability that Jake brought out in her.

He smirked. "Whatever you say."

She knew he could make her eat her words, just prayed that he wouldn't.

"Mama, can I have some juice?" Peter asked, racing over to them.

"It's *may* I, sweetie," Larissa said.

"*May* I have some juice?"

"Sure," she said, going into the kitchen to her oversize bag and pulling out a juice box. She paused in the doorway before returning to the patio. Jake and Peter were in front of the goal net again and this time

Jake was setting himself up as goalie. She watched the two of them together and realized she wasn't the only one who'd been missing a man in her life. No matter the cost to herself, she had to make this new arrangement with Jake work out. For Peter's sake.

"Here's your juice, Peter," Larissa said from the patio.

Jake ruffled Peter's hair, lifting up the boy to carry him back to the patio. It was the first time he'd held his son's small body. A surge of protectiveness roared through him.

This was his son. Peter rested his head on his shoulder and Jake met Larissa's gaze. Something passed between them and he knew she knew what he felt.

"We should get going. Peter needs a nap."

"I'll carry him out to your car. When will you be back?"

"I have to work this afternoon. I won't have time to get our stuff together until after I pick Peter up at the sitter's."

"Can he stay with me?" Jake asked.

"I...I don't know if he would. He doesn't really know you."

"I'm the boy's father. Isn't it time he got to know me?"

"Yes, it is. But watching him takes a lot of patience and attention."

"What do you say, sport?" Jake asked Peter. "Want to stay with me while your mom's at work."

"Are you my dad?" Peter asked.

"I am."

Peter looked at his mom and Larissa took a deep breath and nodded. "It's okay with me, sweetie."

"Can we play soccer some more?"

"After you take a nap," Larissa said.

"Okay, I'll stay with you."

Larissa gathered her things and Jake carried Peter out to her car. She buckled him in the car seat and put Mr. Bear and his blanket around his face.

Jake stood waiting by the car when she turned around. "I'm not due at work until three. I'll bring Peter by around two-thirty."

"Why don't I come to your place for lunch? I can help you pack up your stuff. Peter can help me bring your stuff back here."

"Okay. Are you sure about this living together thing?"

"Yes. I have to do it because I'd feel like less than a man if I didn't."

"Why don't you think about it? I couldn't bear it if you had regrets."

"I wouldn't have asked if I wasn't positive this was the best course of action. Now that I know I have a son, nothing less than living under the same roof will satisfy me."

"Somehow I knew you'd feel that way."

"Knew it this morning or when you first discovered you were pregnant?" he asked.

He still wanted to know why she hadn't come to him to begin with. He would have done the honorable thing then. Even though she'd said she'd wanted to manage motherhood on her own, Larissa wasn't one of those staunch feminists. Sure she'd believed women deserved equal pay and equal opportunity, but she'd always had a sort of dreamy vision of what family life should be.

A vision that included a mother and father and two kids. A cute little cottage on the river. A big yard with room for soccer practice and a dock to fish from. Somehow his vision and hers had blended together in the early-morning hours when they'd talked about the future.

She'd always made him want to talk about the future and maybe he realized that was why her answer now was so important. He wanted to believe that she'd known he would have done the honorable thing three years ago, not because of what society would say, but because of the woman she was.

"I've always known it," she said, quietly.

Without thinking, he reached out and pulled her close in a bear hug. He held her tightly to him and knew deep in his soul he wasn't letting this woman or their son walk out of his life. "I hope this isn't a mistake."

Jake let her go. "It's what's best for Peter. So are you going to stop arguing and move in with me?"

She stared at him. Her eyes were wide and questioning, still holding secrets that he wondered if he'd ever uncover. "I will."

Satisfaction flowed through him. She belonged to him and so did their son. The sooner he had them under his roof the more settled he'd feel. "Good."

She crossed her arms over her chest again and he realized she was trying to put a barrier between them. She didn't realize that running only made him want to chase her. And catch her. His mind filled with images of what he'd do when he caught her. When he coaxed her willingly to his bed.

"I'm going to call Nicola, Uncle Abe's PR person and advise her of this current situation. My folks are going to want to meet their grandson. So after you get off work tonight, we'll head over there, if that's okay with you."

"I'm not sure I want to meet your parents."

"Why not?"

"They're bound to be mad at me."

"They're nicer than I am."

She hadn't even considered the family that Peter would now call his own. Her own dad hadn't spoken to her since she was six and her mom had died during her first year of college, so he'd never had any grandparents. "I doubt that."

"Don't worry about it. I'll take care of everything. Trust me," Jake said.

"You keep saying that."

"I'm going to continue to until you finally believe in me."

"I wish I could, but it's not that easy."

"What's not?"

"Trusting a man."

"I'm not just any man. I'm the father of your child."

"I know," she said. He couldn't know that made it even harder for her to trust him.

Four

After Larissa and Peter left, Jake called his lawyer and had a lengthy conversation to put in motion a bid for custody of Peter. The first thing Marcus had suggested was a paternity test to give them a legal leg to stand on. Jake didn't doubt that Peter was his son. He knew Larissa. And he'd looked into his son's eyes. Peter was his. But he liked the idea of having the documentation to prove it.

Nicola had been out of the office so Jake had left a message for her to call him. Then he drove to Larissa's house. Riverside was a nice suburb of Savannah and as he neared Larissa's house he realized she wasn't just eking out a living. She'd made a life for herself and their son that was comfortable.

He felt a little bad about the plan he had put into motion with Marcus. But he wasn't going to give up his son now that he'd found out about him. Being a father felt right deep in his soul and if he had a few doubts that he wouldn't be up to the job, he'd get over them. There had never been anything he couldn't achieve when he put his mind to it. Except for gaining his father's respect.

Mindful that Larissa said she was going to give Peter a nap, Jake avoided the front door and walked around to the backyard. As he approached the side of the house he heard soft Asian music playing. He rounded the corner to the back of the house and found Larissa lying on a yoga mat in a shady area.

He watched her change poses. He admired her grace and style. But from his position he could also see her cleavage and any altruistic thoughts he had were banished by the rush of desire.

He waited until she finished her routine by sitting in a meditative pose. She looked peaceful and se-rene—untouchable. And she evoked in him a savage-ness he'd always tried to tamp down and hide.

Clearing his throat, he climbed the steps of the deck. Her eyes snapped open and she stared at him. There were beads of perspiration on her neck and chest. His first impulse was to lick them from her skin. His eyes narrowed. His breathing changed and he felt arousal spread throughout his body. Damn.

This reaction to her didn't fit into his well-ordered plans for Larissa.

She scrambled to her feet when she realized he was watching her. The formfitting leggings and snug sleeveless shirt left little of her body to the imagination. It was the first time he'd seen her in anything that wasn't loose and concealing. Even that night they'd made love, she'd insisted they leave the lights low.

Her legs were long and curvy. Her hips a real woman's and not a model's. Her breasts were pert and, he knew from experience, just the right size to nestle in his palms.

The spandex shirt clung to the full globes and Jake had to swallow when her nipples budded against the cloth under his gaze. She stopped moving and he glanced up at her face. A pink blush covered her neck and cheeks, but she didn't cross her arms over her chest.

"Are you sure about this platonic thing?" he asked, his voice husky with need.

"No, I'm not sure."

He took two large steps toward her, closing the gap between them. She didn't smell sweaty the way he did after exercise. It reminded him of how different the two of them were. How different men and women were and how exciting those differences could be.

Unable to resist, he traced with his finger a bead of perspiration that rolled down between her breasts, disappearing under her shirt. She shivered when he reached the border where skin and fabric met. He watched goose bumps spread over her skin and, hesitating only a second, he dipped his finger under her shirt.

She was just as soft to the touch as he remembered. Her breasts appeared a bit bigger than before and he let his finger slide under one of them. She bit her lip and tilted her head to the side, watching him with hooded eyes.

She swayed and he brought his other arm up around her waist, holding her the way he'd dreamed of since he'd opened her car door this morning. He pulled his finger free of her shirt and lifted it to his lips.

Her pupils dilated as she watched him and her breath rushed in and out as if she'd just completed a five-mile run instead of a yoga routine.

The salty taste of her on Jake's tongue only whetted his appetite for more of her. He leaned toward her. She gripped his biceps and rose on her tiptoes. Her breath fanned against his cheek.

He bent and captured her mouth. She opened for him with a sigh that told him she'd needed this embrace as much as he had. Her fingernails bit into his arms as she returned his kiss.

He cupped her bottom and brought her more fully against him. Her hardened nipples pushed into his chest. He swallowed her moan as he deepened their embrace. He reached again for her breast, sliding his hand up under her shirt this time. She shuddered when he palmed a nipple.

He slid his mouth from hers, down the slope of her neck until he could trace the V-neck of her shirt with his tongue. She trembled again in his arms, her hands clutching at his head.

The phone rang inside the house and Larissa pushed him away, stumbling, her eyes wide and wounded. She hurried into the house to take the call and he cursed under his breath. Pivoting on his heel, he walked to the edge of the deck.

He braced his hands on the railing, bowing his head and breathing deeply, searching for his control. Hell, what was he thinking? He hadn't come here to make love to Larissa. In fact, considering their situation it was the last thing he should be doing. Further evidence, as if he needed it, that he wasn't cut out for responsibility. Maybe he should rethink the custody suit. He knew it was male pride motivating him.

He heard her return, sensed her standing in the doorway watching him. She cleared her throat and he glanced over his shoulder at her.

She'd put on a large sweatshirt while she'd been in the house and crossed her arms over her chest. He didn't know what to say to her and he had the feeling if he opened his mouth he'd say something stupid instead of acting like the rather suave guy he liked to think he was.

Finally she said, "Peter's still sleeping. Why don't you come inside and I'll make us some lunch."

"I'm not hungry," he said.

"Oh. Okay."

This wasn't working out the way he'd planned it. "Larissa, sit down."

"Why?"

"We have to talk."

"I guess we do. Are you sure you don't want any food? How about some iced tea?"

"No. Nothing."

She sat down on one of the wrought-iron chairs around a small café-style table. He took one of the chairs, spun it around and sat facing her.

"What'd you want to talk to me about?"

"A couple of things. First off, I'd like to take Peter to get a paternity test."

Larissa laced her fingers together and stared at Jake. He was so familiar to her, yet at the same time a stranger with steely determination. This was the man who'd made D&D's coffeehouse the success it was today. And though Larissa had spent some late nights with Jake in college, he'd been more of a dreamer then than the man he was today.

The calm she'd tried to find through yoga had disappeared as soon as she'd seen Jake. She'd gone into his arms remembering the man she'd left earlier today. The man who'd told her she could trust him. This didn't feel like trust. This felt…this felt like betrayal.

"You don't think he's your son?" she asked at last.

He watched her with that intense dark brown stare that penetrated through the layers she used to protect herself. She flinched under his scrutiny, tucking a stray strand of hair back into her ponytail.

"I didn't say that," he said, running his hands through his thick black curly hair. She could still feel the texture of his hair in her hands. She clenched her hands and tried to concentrate on his words.

"Yes, you did. If you believed me then you wouldn't need a test." She'd known he'd be angry at her for keeping the truth from him but had never expected him to doubt he was the father.

"Don't make this about you and me, Rissa. This is a matter of practicality. I can't provide for Peter until I'm legally recognized as his father. Only a paternity test can prove that."

Practicality. She'd spent a lifetime being practical, realistic and sensible. She understood those things, but just once she wanted the fantasies she still harbored to come true. A million thoughts ran through her head. Jumbled and confused—a chaotic disarray of her view of reality. She pulled her legs up in the chair and wrapped her arms around them. Of all the things that Jake could say to her this was the one thing she'd never expected.

She wished now she'd run away this morning when

Ms. Carmody had called. That she'd taken Peter and disappeared. Anything so she didn't have to go through this. She'd created a mess of complications she'd never considered when she'd kept Peter a secret.

Complications that had made her regret her actions a few times—things like medical history; Peter had asthma. Things like who would take care of her son if she died; Larissa had no family. Things like being a part of a wealthy family; Larissa made enough to provide for her son, but was she denying him the opportunity for more?

"Everything is so…" She trailed off, afraid of revealing too much to Jake. It would be different if they were just friends, if there wasn't that spark of sexual attraction buzzing between them.

He raised one eyebrow at her in question.

"Complex," she said at last.

His lips quirked and he reached across the small table to pull her hands off her legs. He twined their fingers together. "We'll take it one day at a time—together."

Together. The word scared her. She'd grown used to being independent, to being solely responsible for Peter. It was strange to think that Jake would have some say in Peter's life. Not necessarily in a bad way, she realized, which also scared her.

"I'm still not sure that us moving in with you is a good idea."

"Now that I've seen your place, I'd be willing to move here."

She didn't want Jake here in her house. This was her sanctuary from the world. The one place where it didn't matter that she'd never really had a father. "No, we better stay at your house."

"This is a nice place," Jake said after a while, gesturing to the house.

"Thanks. It suits us. We spend a lot of time out here or on the river."

"I never pictured you as an outdoorsy person," he said. He shifted her hands in his, his thumbs making lazy circles on her palms.

"Probably because I'm so bookish."

"Bookish?"

"What would you call me?" she asked.

"Intelligent but in a sexy way."

"I had no idea brains were a turn-on for men."

"I don't know about other men."

She smiled at him, unsure where this was going. She tugged her hands away from his and looked out at the Savannah River. She loved this house even though she'd inherited it from a man she'd scarcely known.

"Did you move here after Peter was born?" he asked.

"Yes, my grandfather left the place to me."

"I'm sorry for your loss."

"That's okay," she said. Her grandfather hadn't

ever spoken to her when he'd been alive. The old man had disowned her mother when she'd first found out she was pregnant. "We weren't close."

"I remember your mom died when we were in college. Do you have any other family?"

"I have Peter."

"This must have been some fun place to explore as a kid."

She shrugged. She'd never visited here until the day they'd moved in. She'd sold her condo in Atlanta and moved here. Her grandfather hadn't kept any pictures of her mom or herself in the house. She'd found a drawer in the mahogany desk in the den filled with unopened letters from her mom. Only one letter had been opened—the one she'd sent to her grandfather telling him he had a great-grandson.

He'd never contacted her, but Larissa often wondered if that was why he'd left her this place. Not for her and for the sins of her mother, but for Peter. The great-grandson he'd never let himself know.

"I know you're an only child, but did you have cousins to play with?" he asked.

"Not every family is like yours, Jake. Some of us are only children of only children."

He put his hands up. "I didn't mean anything by it. This is a great place to raise a son. When you said he only watched PBS, I was scared you were turning him into a little brainiac."

"I'm trying, but he has your genes," she said, trying for a lightness that she didn't really feel.

He grabbed his chest. "Ouch."

She chuckled.

"I'll take that lunch you offered now," he said. Something had changed in his eyes that made a ray of hope blossom in her chest. She realized that there was no one else she'd rather share parenthood with than this man.

Larissa's kitchen reminded him of Tuscany. It was painted rich warm colors. He could tell she'd remodeled since she'd moved in. The houses in this neighborhood had been originally built in the fifties. But her kitchen was very modern. The large butcher-block island where she assembled lunch had a new look to it.

"Is salad okay?"

Not really. He'd still be hungry when he was done. But they'd reached a kind of truce on the deck and he didn't want to rock the boat. "Sure. What can I do to help?"

"Can you cook?"

He laughed. "No. But cutting up veggies isn't that hard."

"No, it's not. I'm making a Greek salad, so you can cut up olives and peppers for it."

She put on a Jimmy Buffett CD while they worked in the kitchen. The first time he'd noticed Larissa in college had been at a Buffett concert. She'd been the only one in their group without a grass skirt or Hawaiian shirt. And she'd turned eight shades of red when Buffett sang "Let's Get Drunk and Screw."

"I love this CD. I remember the first time you heard some of these songs."

"Me, too. I wanted to die, I was so mortified that ya'll were singing it at the top of your lungs."

"Wasn't long before we'd corrupted you and you were singing along. Remember the next concert less than a year later?"

She gave him a saucy grin, one he'd forgotten. For all her shy ways in a large group, one on one, Larissa was a sassy woman. "You always were a bad influence on me."

His track record with women wasn't the best. He'd gotten Larissa pregnant and not known it. In his defense, he'd been going through a lot then. His sister Victoria had disappeared and D&D's was starting to go big time. Jake didn't cut himself any slack for those things. Some men were inherently flawed when it came to women and he was beginning to believe he was one of them.

"Yeah, I guess I was," he said.

He felt her hand on his arm and realized he'd stopped cutting. "I was joking."

He put the knife on the counter, leaning his hip against it and staring down at her. Damn, he'd forgotten how small she was. He felt big—too big for her and for her kitchen. He also felt too hard for the woman who'd blushed at provocative song lyrics. "But there is an element of truth to your words."

She cupped his jaw. Her long fingers were cold against his skin. "Not really. You've never made me do anything I regretted."

There was something in her eyes that convinced him of her sincerity. He leaned down to kiss her. A quick embrace that held shared memories and the hope of finding some sort of peace for the future. She pulled away too soon for him.

"We better get back to work or we'll never eat," she said lightly, stepping away from him and moving around the island.

Did she really think one butcher-block countertop was going to stop him? He'd let her back away earlier when her phone rang but he knew they were going to have to come to terms with this sexual attraction between them before she moved into his place. "Maybe I'm not hungry for rabbit food."

"What are you hungry for?" She tilted her head to the side and watched him with eyes that knew their effect on him.

"Do I really have to tell you?" he asked, coming around the side of the counter and closing the gap between them. He backed her up against the countertop, not stopping until their bodies brushed against each other.

She tipped her head back, exposing her long elegant neck. He lifted one large blunt finger and stroked the length of it. She trembled under his touch and her pulse started to beat more heavily. Her eyes narrowed to slits.

"The only thing on the menu is Greek salad, Jake."

She wasn't ready for anything other than teasing, he thought. Right now, maybe that's all he was ready for too. Marcus had made some interesting points on the phone. A paternity test was only one of the things he wanted from Larissa. He also needed to know why she'd kept her pregnancy a secret.

He stepped away and went back to chopping olives. "Too bad. I had my sights set on something mouthwatering."

She said nothing but assembled the salad and led the way out to the deck overlooking the Savannah River. She was still nervous around him, afraid to trust him, and she was right to be. He had his own plans and she was only a means to an end. As cruel as that sounded, he couldn't curb his gut instinct, which told him an eye for an eye.

"Thanks for lunch," he said while she cleared the plates.

"It was only a salad," she said.

"It was delicious."

"Thanks. I'm not really much of a cook."

"Me either. Luckily I know how to dial for take-out."

"I can't eat take-out every night. And it's really not good for Peter. Or you."

"I run five miles every morning and play soccer on Saturdays."

"I...I've seen you."

"When?"

"Last fall. Peter and I were having a picnic at the park. We were packing up to leave when you guys arrived for your game."

"Why didn't you say something?"

"I was scared."

"Of what?"

"My reasons are personal, Jake."

"Honey, surely not too personal to share with the father of your child."

"Sarcasm doesn't become you."

"Neither do lies you."

"I'm not lying to you."

"Not today, right? It's funny how truth seems to be your ally when you need one."

"Ally? Are we enemies?"

"Only in your eyes."

"When did I make us enemies?"

"When you kept my son a secret," he said savagely.

"I can't believe we're going through this again."

"I'm waiting to hear these reasons of yours, Rissa. Because I have to tell you I can't believe the sweet girl I knew in college would keep this from me. What other secrets are you hiding?"

Five

Larissa stood and walked into her house, unsure what to say but needing to escape. She paused inside the living room. Portraits of Peter lined the wall. She had spent a small fortune in film developing since he'd been born. She'd filled this empty old house with pictures of her son.

With pictures of the small family that she'd finally found. She scanned the pictures, stopping on one taken only two weeks ago, Peter on the dock with his fishing pole in hand. He'd been aggravated that he hadn't caught anything and he stared down into the water with the same determination she'd just seen in Jake's eyes.

She hurried past the photos and entered her kitchen, where she started cleaning. Cleaning had always been a chore that soothed her. It was simple and straightforward, and when she finished she could look back and see what she'd accomplished.

Unlike life, which seemed never to run smoothly. Every time she thought she and Jake had a chance at getting past her deception, his anger reared its ugly head. And she knew he deserved some answers, but the last thing she wanted to do was bare her soul to him.

Jake had always been the one guy she'd wanted. The one guy who'd made her feel like it was okay to be herself. The one guy who…she'd never been able to forget.

She sensed him behind her. She put the rest of the dishes in the dishwasher and turned to face him. He had that bulldog angry look on his face and his arms crossed over his massive chest that told her he wasn't budging until he got some answers.

She swallowed, twisting the dish towel with her hands. "You're right. I do have some secrets that I don't want to share with you."

"I'm trying to understand. But your lack of trust makes it damned hard."

"I know. Remember earlier when you asked me about my grandfather?" she asked, sorting through her past and finding one of the things that seemed safest to tell him. Jake came from a wealthy family with history and pride. And she'd never had a real family until Peter. She'd never felt she'd missed out until she'd had her son and realized what life could've been like.

He leaned against the doorjamb, no less intimidating in the more relaxed pose. "Yes."

His black T-shirt stretched across his chest and she wished she'd never left his arms earlier. He was too handsome for his own good. He could be dirt poor and he'd still have a legion of women after him.

If she'd stayed in his arms earlier, nature would have taken its course and she could have avoided this conversation. But she was vulnerable where Jake was concerned. She didn't want to create any further bonds between them and risk the chance that she'd be hurt when he left. And she knew he'd leave. No man had ever stayed. Starting with her grandfather, before she was even born.

"Well, I never knew him. He and my mom had a falling-out before I was born. He disowned her over her choice of husband."

"Your father?"

She nodded. No way was she ever going to call Reilly Payton her father. The man had made it clear that society may have demanded he do his duty by her mother, but father was one role he'd never wanted to play. She'd legally changed her name to Nielsen when she'd turned 18.

"What's that got to do with you keeping Peter's birth from me?"

She took a deep breath, mentally crossed her fingers and bowed her head. She'd learned early on that if she was going to tell a half-truth it was easier if she wasn't looking the person in the eye. "I didn't want your family to disown you because of me."

"Sweetheart, look at me," he said.

She glanced up at him, hoping he'd let the subject drop. "Yes?"

"That's the biggest whopper I've ever heard. You know Wes and I are brothers and he liked you. My family could care less about your past or where you came from."

She'd forgotten about Jake's college roommate and friend, Wes. Wes was still like a second son to Jake's parents. But she knew that his parents would have minded having a daughter-in-law who'd done the same thing to their son that her mother had done to the Payton boy twenty-five years earlier. And Savannah society would have remembered it too. The Paytons were old money and her parents had been the talk of the town. If there was one thing those Southern ladies liked, it was scandal and gossip. Larissa had decided long ago she'd had her fill of being fodder for them.

"I'm sorry. The truth is my mom got pregnant to trap my…" She didn't know what to call the man who'd married her mom and then refused to have anything to do with the child they'd created. Certainly not father. Never father.

"…her boyfriend into marriage. I couldn't do that to you."

Jake cursed savagely under his breath. He pushed his hands through his hair and watched her. He entered the kitchen, walking toward her with a slowly measured gait. He stopped when there was about six inches of space between them. But she still felt dwarfed by his physical presence. She tried to step back, but the counter stopped her.

"Did you get pregnant on purpose?" he asked her.

She couldn't gauge his mood. Suddenly she felt very small and awkward. Wrapping her arms around her waist, she stared at his chest and whispered, "No, I'd never do that."

Jake took her chin in his large, warm hand, tipping her head back until their eyes met. "Then why would I think you had trapped me?"

She couldn't think when his breath brushed over her cheek like that. When his eyes looked down on her with a tenderness she'd thought never to see in them again. When he pulled her into his embrace and wrapped his arms around her. Oh, God, this was what she'd been afraid of. Leaning on Jake felt right in the seat of her soul and she knew that he wouldn't stay, but she couldn't help herself.

Didn't want to step away. They didn't move from

each other's arms until Peter came into the kitchen, rubbing the sleep from his eyes.

Her heart was heavy with fears and hope swirled together. She wanted to believe the promise Jake offered her, but she feared as soon as she did, she'd end up getting hurt.

Jake sat on the couch with Peter reading Jake's favorite book *Lord of the Rings: Fellowship of the Rings* to him. Peter was fascinated by the world of Middle-earth and was rapt in his attention.

Jake glanced at the mantel clock. What was taking Larissa so long? "I'm going to check on your mom. Do you want to watch some TV?"

"Yes, please, Daddy," Peter said with a smile.

They'd had a lot of fun this afternoon together. He and Larissa had told Peter that Jake was his father. Peter had been overjoyed at the news and had started calling him "Daddy" almost immediately. He said the word so often, Jake realized how much his son had missed having a father.

Jake turned the television on and left his son watching *Arthur*. Larissa had provided a long list of acceptable television programs on a laminated four-by-six-inch card for Jake when they'd moved in. He also had cards on acceptable words to use—apparently *shut up, stupid* and *idiot* were forbidden, as well as every curse word. There was an approved food list, which Jake had noticed was lacking his favorite cereal. He'd added it to the list with a Sharpie pen and put it on the kitchen counter where she'd see it when she fixed breakfast tomorrow morning.

He went down the hall to the guest bedroom he'd given Larissa. He didn't question it, but there was a sense of rightness to having her under his roof. And for him being responsible for her and their son.

It felt right in his gut. He sensed this was what his father must feel when the entire family was assembled at their home. It was the first time he'd ever felt anything in common with his dad and it felt…weird.

He rapped on her door. "You ready?"

"I don't know," she opened the door, and nervously stepped back.

"How do I look?" she asked.

She looked too damned good to be someone's mom. Her dress was a feminine bit of silk that teased him with its demureness. Teased him with the hint of sexuality beneath that flounced skirt ending just above the knees and the scoop neckline that hinted at her cleavage.

"You look fine."

"Just fine?" she asked, hurrying back over to the mirror and patting her hair once more.

"What's wrong with fine?" he asked, lounging against the door frame. He was fascinated to see the normally unflappable Larissa so unsure of herself. He'd never known her to worry about what she was going to wear.

"I'm meeting your family for the first time. Plus I'm bringing scandal down on them. I think I should look better than fine."

She did, but he wasn't going to reveal anything more to her. Her features were drawn and she looked more nervous now than she had in the doctor's office earlier when they'd had the paternity test done.

He left the doorway and entered the room. The bed was piled with discarded clothing. He wondered if this went back to what she'd said the other day about her grandfather. How did knowing your family had rejected you before you were born affect someone? For all his problems with his father, he knew the old man loved him and would always be there for him.

"What's this all about, Rissa?"

She sighed and sank down on the clothes strewn on the double bed. "I don't want to go."

He sat down next to her. Her perfume was faintly floral and sexy to him. But then everything about Larissa was. He reached for her hands, which she had clenched tightly into fists on her lap. He pried her hands open and held them loosely in his own.

She tipped her head to the side and looked up at him. It was a beseeching look that made him want to give her whatever she asked for. But at the same time, they were in this predicament because of her actions. He lifted one eyebrow in silent question.

She licked her lips and then turned her head toward

her lap again. "It was hard enough telling you about Peter. I don't think I can face your family."

"There's no other choice. You have to go with me so we both know how to handle the media. Nicola was clear on that point."

"I wish Jasmine Carmody had never called me," she said, looking up at him again.

"I'm glad she did despite the trouble she's caused. Jasmine Carmody has given me my son."

Larissa said nothing, but her eyes revealed the truth. And the truth wasn't a pretty and nice thing. It was that this woman would have rather run away than face him with the news of his own son.

He cursed under his breath and stood, walking away from her. Every time he thought he'd forgiven her, he was reminded he hadn't. Spending two hours in the toy store with his son had gone a long way toward showing him what he'd missed out on all these years. And now she was telling him again that she regretted telling him the truth.

He clenched his fists and walked toward the front door. "Get your purse, Larissa. We're leaving."

"Jake…"

He didn't pause or turn to look at her. She'd made her decisions. Now he'd made his. He'd see Marcus tonight at Crofthaven and set the custody suit in motion. It was obvious to him, no matter what Larissa said, she couldn't be trusted where Peter was concerned.

He was willing to cut her a little slack because of her upbringing, and he understood that she'd had a rough shake early in life. But Jake wasn't responsible for another man's mistakes and he wasn't going to keep paying for them.

Her hand on his arm stopped him and he pivoted to face her.

"I'm sorry," she said suddenly.

He realized she was trying to tell him something else. But he'd never been good at reading minds and didn't think he was suddenly going to get better at it.

"For?"

"Everything."

"Don't be sorry for everything. That's too big a burden for your shoulders. We're both responsible for this mess and I'm not going to let you continue to carry it alone."

Larissa felt small and very out of place in the grand foyer of Crofthaven. Peter leaned closer to her and she stooped to pick up her son as Jake gave their coats to Joyce Jones, the housekeeper. Jake exchanged pleasantries with the woman and then cupped his hand under Larissa's elbow, leading her down the hall.

"Where are we going?" Larissa asked.

"To the library. Relax."

"I can't. This place is intimidating."

"It's just a house," he said.

"It's not just a house. It's a historical landmark. It's your family's mark on Savannah and I feel like an interloper."

"Relax," he said again. "I didn't grow up here."

He rubbed Peter's head and their son glanced up at him. "Ready to meet your family?"

Peter didn't answer, just stuck his thumb in his mouth and held tighter to her neck. "Maybe I should have gotten a sitter."

"We don't need a sitter," he said. "What a couple of cowards you two are."

"Am not," Peter said, squirming in her arms to be put down. "I'm just as brave as Frodo."

Jake ruffled his son's hair. "I knew you were."

Peter glanced up at Larissa. "Mommy's not so brave."

"Then we'll be brave for her," Jake said, stooping down to Peter's eye level.

Peter nodded and slipped his hand into hers. He gripped hers tightly and smiled up at her. And she felt an infusion of love for her son and for his father. Jake was taking this task of being a father very seriously and she regretted that she'd waited so long to let him know he was a dad.

"Ready?" Jake asked.

She nodded and followed Jake into the library. The librarian in her was in awe. Private collections like this one were the stuff dreams were made of. She almost forgot her nerves. Despite his courageous words in the hall, Peter seemed to have picked up on her apprehension and now clung to her leg. She rubbed his back, focusing on Peter and not the others in the room.

There were five people in the room. Jake's uncle, Abraham Danforth, and Wesley Brooks were at the computer desk on the far side of the room. She knew Wes from college, "Honest" Abe from the articles she'd read in the newspaper about him and his family. Abe was the patriarch of the Danforths, a retired Navy Seal who was currently running for the senate.

There was a couple on the couch who stood when they entered. They had to be Jake's parents. There was too much emotion in their gazes for them not to be. They both eyed her and Peter with curiosity. The other woman with gorgeous red hair and bright green eyes was taller than she was and Larissa was no shorty at five-seven. She had to be Abe's PR manager.

"Is this our grandson?" Miranda Danforth asked, crossing the room. Jake's mom had blond hair worn in a sleek bob. Her eyes were a warm blue that made Larissa feel safe and comfortable.

"Mom, this is Larissa Nielsen and my son," Jake said.

Peter clung tighter to Larissa and wouldn't turn around and meet his grandmother at first. "I'm sorry," she said. "He's not used to meeting new people."

"That's okay," Miranda said, running her hand

down Peter's back. ''Why don't you come sit down with me?''

Larissa followed her across the room, conscious of all the others there. Wes Brooks, Jake's college roommate, looked up from the desk where he was working on the computer. He gave her a friendly smile and a wink. Larissa smiled back. She knew Jake's not officially adopted brother from their college days. And it was nice to see a familiar face in this sea of Danforths.

Miranda seated herself on a leather sofa and Larissa sank down next to her, pulling Peter onto her lap. Harry Danforth stood on the other side of the room. Jake had followed them and he sat on the other side of Larissa. He dropped his arm over her shoulders and she felt comforted by his presence.

As he'd said earlier, she wasn't alone in carrying this burden. But Peter had never felt like a burden to her. He'd always been her joy. And these people, Jake's clan, were lucky to have her precious son in their family.

''Jake called me earlier about your situation—'' Nicola said.

''Pardon me for interrupting, Nicola,'' Miranda Danforth said. ''Peter, would you like to come to the kitchen with me for some cookies and milk?''

Peter lifted his head from Larissa's shoulder. ''What kind?''

''Peter.''

"That's okay, Larissa. Double chocolate chunk, I believe."

"Mama?"

"You can go, sweetie. Mrs. Danforth is your grandmother."

"Wow. A daddy and a grandmother."

Miranda smiled down at him. "You've got a grandfather as well as a bunch of other family."

"Really?" Peter asked.

"Really," she said. "I'll tell you all about them while we have our cookies and milk."

"Okay!" Peter said, taking Miranda's offered hand and following her from the room.

Larissa felt naked without her little boy on her lap. She laced her fingers together and tried not to pretend that she was the cause of an uncomfortable situation for this very important family.

"I've been thinking about this all afternoon and I've come up with a solution that I think will take the heat out of anything Ms. Carmody writes."

"Great, I'll help in any way I can," Larissa said.

Jake rubbed her shoulder, and she leaned back to smile at him. He didn't smile at her, but a warmth entered his eyes that made her acutely aware of every place where their bodies touched.

"Perfect. I think you two need to get married as soon as possible."

Jake surged to his feet. "No way."

For Larissa, the next few moments seemed to happen in slow motion and there was a ringing in her ears. She wasn't sure what she'd expected, but being forced to marry the man whose child she'd had wasn't it. She had the first inkling of what her mother may have felt all those years ago when she'd faced Reilly Payton and his family—trapped and doomed.

"Excuse me," she said, standing. She walked from the room, down the long hall and out into the night.

Any chance of forever happiness with Jake was gone in an instant, because no man could ever love a woman who'd forced him into a marriage he didn't want.

Six

Jake knew he'd screwed up even before he'd felt Larissa leave the room. But one look at the condemnation shining from his father's eyes was all it took to make him feel about fourteen again. Dammit.

He turned away from his father and focussed instead on Nicola.

"Is a marriage going to be a problem?" she asked.

Jake had no idea. He suspected that he was the last man Larissa would marry right now, after hearing his reaction to the suggestion. But the suggestion had taken him completely off guard.

"No, it won't be a problem, will it, Jacob?" His father, Harry Danforth, said. There were maybe two moments in his life when Jake had felt as if he'd pleased the old man. Once when he was six and won the all-city soccer kickoff, and once when he had made his first million with D&D's Coffeehouses. But for the remainder of Jake's life, he'd seen his father with the same look he had on his face now: one of disappointment.

Even Uncle Abe and Wes were looking at him like he'd screwed up. But he knew what his father meant. He'd made this mess, now it was time to clean it up.

"I don't know that Larissa wants to marry me," Jake said. Not much of an excuse but the only one he had.

"Then convince her," Harry said.

"I'll try." Jake stood and exited the room. He paused in the hallway and leaned back against the wall. His hands were shaking and he had that gut feeling that life was changing in a way he hadn't anticipated.

The hallways were lit with wall sconces and Jake figured Larissa hadn't gone out the front door, but out the back into the gardens. He pushed away from the wall and moved slowly through the house. Crofthaven was a showplace, unlike his parents' more modest house.

He stepped out into the spring evening and paused. What if he couldn't convince Larissa to marry him? He'd learned a long time ago that running away from problems wasn't a solution. But marriage? It wasn't as if he had anything against the institution, but he wasn't sure it was the right move for them.

He heard the rustling of leaves and a soft fall of footsteps. He followed the sound until he found Larissa. She was walking around one of the smaller formal gardens in the backyard. Hedges surrounded it and there was a very European feel to this garden. A marble bench was tucked off to one side and Larissa paused next to it, then sank down on the bench. He stayed in the shadows to watch her.

The full moon and landscape lanterns provided soft lighting to the area, revealing the woman who was bound to him in ways he didn't understand. It was more than that they shared a child. It was more than sharing college memories. It was a soul-deep feeling that made him flinch and that he found difficult to ignore.

He didn't know what to say to her. He wasn't really sure what he wanted from her. But he knew what duty demanded and he'd give it his best shot.

He was about to step from the shadows, when Larissa turned her head to the right and brought the blossom of a hibiscus close to her face, inhaling deeply. What was she thinking?

''Can I join you?'' he asked.

She turned toward him. He stepped from the shadows and waited for her permission to join her.

She shrugged and crossed her arms over her chest. He sat next to her, leaving space between them.

Though it was only a few inches, he knew the gap here was miles wide. His next words would have to build a bridge over it. But he wasn't ready. He was still angry that she'd never told him about Peter before now. He knew he needed to get past the anger and thought he'd been making some progress in that direction.

But sitting in his uncle's library and knowing those closest to him knew the mother of his child didn't think he was good enough to be a father—well, hell, it hurt. And he'd reacted the only way he'd ever learned—by lashing out and hurting back.

Hurting the one woman he wanted to protect. She looked fragile sitting here in the garden. But he knew she wasn't fragile. Larissa was a survivor. She rolled with the punches and kept plodding along with life.

She cleared her throat. "I'm sorry I ran out like that. I…"

Suddenly everything was clear and he knew, despite the anger and need for vengeance still pulsing through him, that marriage to Larissa wasn't just a right choice; it was a necessity.

"I'm sorry."

"It's okay. I know you don't want to marry me."

"The thing is, I'm not sure I don't."

"What are you saying?"

"I wasn't prepared to have everyone know you thought so little of my fathering skills."

"Oh, Jake, I didn't."

"Of course, you did."

"Didn't you hear anything I said to you earlier?"

"About what?"

"My family. I never thought about you as a father, Jake. I thought about you as a man trapped by circumstance. And I was right, wasn't I?"

He cursed under his breath and stood, then paced away from her. He was a man trapped, but not so much by circumstance as by his past. By all the lousy decisions he'd made to get to this point. All the time when he'd put feeling good and having fun in front of responsibility.

It was time to get his act together in his personal life and he knew it.

He turned back to Larissa, who watched him with wide, wet eyes. He knew he'd hurt her. Somehow he hadn't expected her pain to cut him. But it did.

He strode back to her and took her hands in his. He sank down in front of her on one knee and looked up into those pretty blue eyes. Those eyes that usually showed her wit and intelligence, but tonight were guarded and vulnerable.

"Larissa Nielsen, will you marry me?"

Larissa wasn't sure what to say. Marrying Jake, well honestly, it was what she'd been secretly dreaming of since she'd first met him in college. But she'd also dreamed they'd have a huge wedding in Savannah so the old gossips wouldn't be able to talk. She'd wear an elaborate white gown similar to Princess Di's and she'd be the most beautiful woman on that day.

It was a fantasy she'd devoted too much time thinking about. Despite Jake being down on bended knee, Larissa knew that responsibility was motivating Jake and not love or eternal devotion. And she knew that he was a good man. He'd already proved he could be a good father. And sometimes in life you had to take what was offered and kiss goodbye the secret dreams you'd harbored.

"Are you going to keep me hanging forever?" he asked, his voice low and husky. When she looked into those devastating dark brown eyes of his, she wondered if she'd ever be able to deny him anything.

She shook her head. He was doing his duty—darn it. She had to remember Jake was still angry with her for keeping Peter a secret for three years. Jake wasn't in love with her, and no matter what else happened, she had to protect her emotions from him. Because she knew from watching her mother's bitter experience that falling in love with an illusion was never a good thing.

"You don't have to do this," she said at last, forcing herself to look away from him. She looked instead out at the well-tended gardens. She and her mom had had a window box at the small duplex they'd lived in most of her life. One small box that they'd filled with annuals every year. And though Crofthaven wasn't Jake's childhood home, she knew this kind of garden—the kind that took a small army to maintain—was what he was used to.

Their lives were worlds apart and she wondered in her heart if they could ever make anything work between them. Even his original idea of them living together now seemed doomed. But marriage—marriage was sacred to her because she knew that when it wasn't right, too many people got hurt. Innocent little people that had no right being hurt by choices that adults made.

"Do what?" he asked, shifting closer to her on the ground. His arms circled her hips and tugged her closer to him. He didn't leave any space between them. She remembered what it was like to be in his arms and wanted to be there again. She'd never thought of herself as sex crazed until she met Jake. He made all her senses go on hyperalert.

He was so close and she remembered their earlier embraces. She still ached for him in this most basic way. She needed something from him that she wasn't sure she should take, because it would make her even more vulnerable.

"The down-on-one-knee proposal thing."

"It's for me as much as for you."

"Yeah, right. I heard you in the library, Jake. You don't want to marry me."

"Dammit, Rissa, you piss me off," he said, pinching her butt.

She swatted his hand away. "I know I do. So why are you asking me to marry you."

He wriggled his eyebrows at her. "You also turn me on."

"Is this a joke to you?" she asked.

He cursed under his breath and then hugged her tightly. "I can't explain it, but there's something about you I've never been able to forget."

Her heart melted a little at his words. He let go of her hands and cupped her face, bringing her face toward his. He brushed his lips over hers, softly, gently...seductively. Making her yearn for deeper contact between them. But she knew what he was doing, what he was trying to say with this kiss. And she returned it. Took control of the embrace, kissing him deeply.

Jake stayed at her feet and it was a heady feeling to dominate him. He was totally at her mercy. His head tipped up to hers; his body was under hers. Her emotions swirled out of control. She wanted more from him than this. She wanted—no, needed—something that he wasn't offering.

Something more than duty. She broke the kiss, taking deep breaths to try to remember that despite the garden and the moonlight, this wasn't a love story. She wasn't the heroine in some happily-ever-after tale. Reality was that Jake hadn't wanted to marry her. It was only the pressure of the media and his family that had sent him out after her.

And despite his sweet words, she knew it was too soon for Jake to feel anything but anger toward her.

"What's going through that head of yours, Rissa?"

"Nothing you'd want to hear."

"I know I've screwed up one thing after another, but marry me and let me make this right."

"If we got married it'd be more business than romance, wouldn't it?"

"It would be what we made it. There's no one else in our relationship but us and Peter."

"I'm scared, Jake."

"Of what?"

"Of making the wrong decision and ruining Peter's life."

"I told you earlier that those shoulders of yours are too small to carry everything. Share that burden with me, Rissa, I'm not going to let you down again."

Promise? She wanted to ask but didn't. Normally she wasn't this needy. Normally she wasn't this timid. Normally she made her decisions and lived with the consequences. But it was time to stop clinging to girlhood fantasies and start living in the real world. A world that included more than her and Peter.

"Okay, Jake. I'll marry you."

Jake figured it probably wasn't the best acceptance in history, but he knew it was good enough for him. He stood, pulled Larissa to her feet and took her in his arms.

But her fingers over his lips stopped him. "No, Jake."

"Why not?"

"I want this marriage to work for Peter's sake."

"I've never heard that sex screwed up a marriage."

"I think it would screw up ours. I can't think straight when you kiss me."

"Good," he said, lowering his head again. But she turned away from him and his lips barely brushed her hair.

"Dammit, woman."

"You're not listening to me."

"You're not saying anything I want to hear."

"I'm sorry, but I think keeping things platonic between us is for the best."

"Woman, who are you kidding?"

"Maybe myself. But it's important to me."

"Hell," he said, letting her go. She took a step away from him, but it didn't change the way his blood was racing. He was still aroused and could tell from her shallow breathing and flushed skin she was too. If he pushed her, he could convince her she was wrong. He knew it. And he suspected she knew it.

Why then was she saying no?

"I'm not letting this go. Honestly, I don't think we can live together without sleeping together."

"You may be right. But I'd like us to try it."

"I don't understand."

"It's because we have to get married," she said softly.

He waited, sensing there was more she had to say. Here was the Larissa he'd known in college. The quiet and contemplative woman who'd spent hours discussing world politics but had never said a word about her upbringing. Would he ever understand this woman?

Finally she bit her bottom lip and looked up at him. "I don't want to start thinking there's more between us than obligation."

He knew she was being serious. He wanted to respond to that, to take this discussion even deeper, but instead, all he could think about was her lips. The bottom one she kept nibbling on as she thought about what she was going to say next. He wanted to suckle on it, to tease away her solemn mood with a lighter one. A safer one. Because he didn't like where this conversation was going.

"More? Like what?" he asked at last.

She crossed her arms over her chest and tipped her head to the side, watching him with those wide expressive eyes of hers. "Like love."

Oh, no, not love. If the topic didn't change soon, he'd have to say to hell with it and force matters back into the physical realm, where he was more confident. "Just love?"

"The in-sickness-and-in-health, until-death-do-us-part stuff. I don't want to buy into this fantasy that I've had in my head for so long a time.''

"What fantasy?'' Did he have a starring role in this image in her head or was he a walk-on replacement? He suspected the latter.

"Oh, Jake. Don't make me tell you this.''

He held his hands up. Far be it for him to force anything from her. "I'm not making you tell me anything.''

"I know. Let's go inside and tell Peter we're getting married.'' She started walking out of the garden. Jake wasn't really ready to rejoin his family. Even though he'd convinced Larissa to marry him, he knew his dad still wouldn't be pleased.

"I'm not sure how much he understands,'' Jake said, letting her change the subject.

"He's pretty smart for his age. But you're right, I don't think he realizes we aren't married.''

She kept walking and he had no choice but to follow her. Dammit, when had he become a coward? He took her elbow and led her up the path to the house. "He took to me being his dad really well.''

"I'm sure the two shopping carts of toys you bought him didn't hurt.''

"Hey, the kid had never been to Toys "R" Us, Rissa. I think that constitutes neglect,'' he said. Jake had never been to one, either. He and Peter had enjoyed their afternoon in the store immensely.

She pulled away from him and stopped. "Peter's not neglected."

"Hey, I was kidding. You've done a great job with our son. I'm proud to call him my boy."

"Sorry about that. Must be the single mom in me."

"Well, you're not a single parent anymore."

"No, I'm not. That's going to take some adjusting for all of us. And for all his easygoing nature, you wouldn't believe how stubborn he can be about things."

"Sure I would. He's your son."

"I'm not stubborn."

"What would you call it?"

"Determined," she said with a faint smile.

They'd reached the house, but she didn't enter. She stood there with her hands twisted together and waited.

He pulled her close for a quick hug and then opened the door to the house. Even though he'd never had any trouble sweet-talking women, suddenly he couldn't find the right words to use with Larissa. He was out of his element here and he didn't like it.

He led her back into the library. His folks were sitting on the floor with Peter, helping him put together a puzzle. Standing with Larissa at his side and watching his parents and son together, Jake felt like everything in his world had finally come together.

Seven

Larissa was glad to leave Crofthaven behind. She'd put Peter in the new car seat in Jake's big Suburban while he went to have a few last words with his father and Wes. It was odd to see Jake and Wes at Crofthaven, but they fit in there in a way she'd never imagined.

Nicola had recommended a Vegas wedding and would contact a few of the bridal magazines to come and photograph her for their spreads. Jake had taken over when they'd reentered the living room and she'd been happy to take a back seat to him. This whole marriage thing still felt very surreal.

She knew she was never going to sleep tonight.

Too much had happened and she needed·time to herself to figure it out. She'd never imagined that having a child with a man could make things so complicated. There were some papers she had to sign before they were married. The family lawyer, Jake's cousin Marcus, had recommended she get her lawyer to read them. Unlike the Danforths, she didn't have a lawyer. But she had a friend from college who'd become one.

According to Marcus, the papers were straightforward—your run-of-the-mill prenuptial agreement without too many complications. She understood why Jake had wanted a paternity test after reading it. Jake had more money and assets that she'd ever imagined.

She rubbed the bridge of her nose. She felt she was getting a migraine. She took Mr. Bear from her purse and tucked him into the car seat with Peter.

Though the hour was late, Peter was still awake. Meeting his family hadn't intimidated him at all. He was practically buzzing with excitement. She sat next to him in the back seat of the car.

"Did you know my daddy has two brothers and two sisters?" he asked her.

She pushed his hair back from his eyes. "Yes, I did."

"But one of my aunts is missing."

Victoria. Jake had told her a little bit about it earlier. They'd found a body in the attic at Crofthaven and the family refused to believe the remains might be Vicky's. But so far no proof had been offered. "I'd heard that as well."

"My grandmother—she said I could call her Granny—told me all about them."

"I'm glad. Do you like having all this family?"

"I guess. I'm tired, Mama."

"I know, sweetie. Why don't you close your eyes?" she suggested. He leaned against the side of his car seat. She had the idea it was going to take him a long time to settle down.

"Are they always going to be our family?" he asked.

She wondered at that. But she knew Jake well enough to know that he wasn't going to let Peter out of his life now that he'd found him. "They'll always be your family, kiddo."

"What about you?" he asked. He reached for her hand and she gave it to him. He tucked it between his face and the car seat, leaning on her hand.

Though the angle was awkward, she didn't pull her hand back. She loved these moments when he just needed to be touching her. "What about me?"

"Aren't they your family?" he asked.

Family. It was the one thing that had always eluded her. She'd created her own little safe unit with Peter, but anything larger scared her. "I guess so. When your daddy and I get married, they will be my family, too."

"What's married?" Peter asked as Jake opened the door and climbed behind the wheel.

"I'll explain more in the morning."

"Okay, Mama."

"You want to climb up front with me?" Jake asked.

"Sure," she said. She leaned over and kissed Peter whose eyes were finally beginning to droop. She got out of the car and moved to the front seat.

As she closed the passenger door, she heard Peter's sleepy voice. "Thanks, Daddy."

"What for?"

"For my family."

Larissa felt a pain deep in her heart. Of all the gifts that Jake had given Peter, he wasn't impressed with the money he'd spent at the toy store. He'd been impressed by the one thing she'd never been able to give him. And it hurt to realize that she'd been depriving him of it all along because of her own fears.

"You're welcome, buddy," Jake said, his voice low and husky. He reached into the back seat and ruffled Peter's hair.

They started the car and drove back toward Savannah in silence. Larissa's thoughts troubled her. She'd never thought of herself as selfish, never realized that she'd put her needs in front of her son's. She never acknowledged that the fear she'd always secretly harbored had driven her to isolate herself from others.

"I know this is kind of rushed, but I promise we'll have a nice wedding."

She knew Jake was trying to ease her mind. But she was having a hard time acknowledging her past behavior and dealing with the guilt it now caused her. "I'm sure whatever you decided on will be fine."

He turned to look at her, his features stark in the dashboard lights. "I want it to be better than fine, Larissa."

She hugged herself, feeling more vulnerable than ever, even more so than when she'd given birth to Peter alone in the hospital. "I'm not sure I deserve that."

"Why not?" he asked. He'd turned his attention back to the road and she was glad. She didn't want him to look at her.

"I just suddenly feel very selfish."

He didn't say anything, and she waited until they'd driven at least a mile before she spoke again. "I've been so afraid of getting hurt that I didn't think of Peter."

"You said it earlier—he's not neglected."

"Who's to say what constitutes neglect? I'd never realized how my own fears were shaping him. He really took to your mom."

"Yes, he did. She took to him, too. She offered to watch him when we go to Vegas," Jake said.

"I'm sure he'd love that."

"Good. That's settled." He reached across the seat

and took her hand, holding it in his for a minute before placing it on his thigh. She felt reassured in ways she shouldn't because she'd promised herself that she wouldn't let herself care for Jake.

It was more important than ever that she make this marriage work. If she didn't, then they'd all end up hurt. And she wasn't going to be responsible for causing the men she loved any more pain.

It was midnight a week later and Jake was wide-awake. So he got out of his bed and wandered down the hall to the kitchen. He tried to pretend it was family concerns that disturbed him. Wes had been out at Crofthaven all week trying to stop a computer virus that Uncle Abe had downloaded with his e-mail. His father hadn't called once but Jake knew the old man was disappointed. His mom had dropped by twice and Larissa had disappeared each time.

Too much had happened lately. It wasn't every day that he found out he had a son. And that was partly the reason for his restlessness. But he knew the true reason was the sweet blonde sleeping in the room next to his.

Larissa was more of a woman than he remembered. It wasn't as if he'd forgotten her in the almost four years since he'd last seen her. She'd always elicited a blend of bittersweet memories. He'd thought he'd scared her away that long-ago night with his love-making. Larissa had always been so innocent—having a one-night stand would have been enough to scare her.

He opened the fridge and stared at the contents. Larissa had brought groceries on her way home. He reached past the soy milk and grabbed the six-pack of Coors that had been pushed to the back of the fridge. He took the six-pack outside. He stretched out on one of the loungers, feeling the moisture that had developed from the night air saturate his T-shirt. He pulled it off and tossed it on the ground next to the beer.

Tipping his head back, he watched the stars. He remembered one time when Larissa had talked him into going to the observatory. They'd spent the night listening to *Dark Side of the Moon* and watching constellations.

Damn, that was a long time ago. Sometimes he felt years older than he was.

He heard the scrape of footsteps on the ground and turned to see Larissa silhouetted in the doorway. She wore a nightshirt that buttoned down the front. It wasn't meant to be sexy even though it did leave her long legs bare, but he found it so. To distract himself he took a long draw on his beer bottle. As a distraction, it was a piss poor one.

Jimmy Buffett had the right idea when he'd written ''Why Don't We Get Drunk and Screw.'' Just mindless sex with Larissa was what he needed tonight. But he knew in the morning it would have consequences.

He ached for her. And having her here in his house made that ache deepen. He'd never had a woman here overnight. With all the traveling he'd done in recent years, there really hadn't been time for a relationship. Hell, that was an excuse. He could have had a woman the night before and he'd still want Larissa with this gut-twisting need.

He knew he wasn't going to sleep or have anything resembling comfort until they'd spent a few hours in bed together. But he'd agreed to a platonic marriage. He intended to try to honor it.

"Can I join you?" she asked. Her hair hung in waves around her shoulder, tousled and disheveled from sleep. He knew she was a natural blonde, but there were so many different shades in her hair that he used to suspect she dyed it. But dying her hair wasn't something that Larissa would do. She was always very genuine.

"Sure. You want a beer?" he asked, gesturing to the six-pack at his feet.

She shook her head and hesitated near his chair. "Are you getting drunk?"

What would she do if he was? "Nah. Just passing time."

"Are you okay?" she asked. She glanced around for somewhere to sit. The other chairs were damp with moisture. She picked his shirt up from the ground and used it to wipe down the seat of one of the lounge chairs. She dragged it closer to his lounger and put her feet on the bottom of his.

Such small, feminine feet. His looked big and rough next to hers. He wanted to explore all the ways they were different. To strip them both naked and take his time with the exploration.

"Why wouldn't I be okay?" he asked, to distract himself from her sweetly curved body and the images of her body dancing in his head. One night years ago wasn't enough.

"Well, it's after midnight and you're sitting in the dark drinking. Something about that doesn't seem like the confident man I've come to know." She ran her toe up his calf, teasing him. Her toenails were painted a deep luscious red that confirmed what he already knew. There was more to the prim librarian than she wanted the world to see.

He glanced up and realized she'd been watching him stare at her legs. "I can't sleep."

She ran her toes back down his leg and then tucked her feet under her and tilted her head to the side. "Why not?"

"You don't want to know," he said, draining his bottle of beer. He leaned over to replace it in the carton and get a fresh one. He twisted the cap off and offered it to her.

She reached forward and took the bottle. Her shirt gaped open and he had a glimpse of the inner curve of her breast. His body hardened a little more, and he shifted his legs to find a more comfortable position.

She took a long sip of the beer and then handed the bottle back to him with a smile. "I wouldn't have asked if I didn't want to know what was keeping you awake."

"I'm hard with wanting you," he said baldly.

"Oh."

"I had a feeling you'd say that. Go back to bed, Larissa, before I forget my good intentions and seduce you."

She stood up and he felt a twinge of disappointment. "Who seduced whom the last time?"

She walked away before he could respond to her. And he watched the smooth swaying of her hips.

Larissa double-checked her seat belt and waved goodbye to Peter in Miranda Danforth's arms as they drove away. Ten days had passed since she'd let Jake know he was Peter's dad. Tears burned the back of her eyes and she stared out the window until she had her emotions under control. Jake drove away from his parents' home through Savannah and headed to the airport.

Jake's family home was just as luxurious as Croft-haven, but a little smaller in scale. It was also homier. The walls in the family room had been covered with pictures of Jake and his siblings at various ages. And there was a display that was practically a shrine to the trophies Jake had won playing soccer.

"What happened with Victoria?"

"She disappeared at a concert."

"When?"

"Years ago. We all feel responsible. She was our baby…"

"You can't protect everyone."

"I know. I just—I bought her those tickets, Rissa. *Me*. The big brother who always spoiled her."

"It's not your fault."

She waited for him to elaborate, but he didn't. He'd been like this since they'd gotten up this morning. Was he having second thoughts? She wouldn't blame him if he did—she had a few doubts herself that this marriage was the right thing to do.

"Have you changed your mind about our wedding?" she asked.

He fiddled with the radio dial, tuning in a rock station. "No."

He turned the volume up and Three Doors Down sang about being Superman. She tried to relax against the leather seat, but she couldn't. She tried to tell herself that this marriage wasn't their kryptonite, but it felt like it.

She tried to tell herself it was the fact that she was leaving the Southeast, something she'd never done before. She tried to tell herself it was the fact that she'd left Peter with her soon-to-be in-laws. She tried to pretend it had absolutely nothing to do with the man sitting next to her.

"I've never been out of Georgia, really. I mean, I've been to Hilton Head, but that's practically Georgia, it's so close."

He didn't turn the volume down or even glance her way. She remembered last night when he'd put her hand on the top of his thigh. "You're rambling."

"Yes, I am. I wonder why?" she asked. She wanted to touch him again. Even though they had an early flight, he'd still taken time to go for a run this morning. His legs were muscled and solid. Her fingers tingled with the remembered feel of his leg under her touch.

"Nervous?" he suggested.

"I wasn't until you started acting like some darned robot this morning."

"Robot?" His tone was disinterested. He'd practically ignored her at his parents' house.

"Listen, Jake, I'm not in the mood to play word games with you. If this is what our married life is going to be like I don't think we should go through with it."

He turned the radio off and removed his sunglasses, glancing over at her. There was something unreadable in his eyes that warned her that he was not in a pleasant mood. "It's too late for that."

"No, it's not."

He didn't say anything else and Larissa knew she

should have remembered the lesson she'd learned a long time ago. That she couldn't really depend on anyone but herself. Despite what he said, she knew her shoulders were strong enough to carry the burden of single-parenthood. She wanted to take Peter and her grandfather's Bayliner and take to the sea. They would find a place where the two of them could live together—maybe an island somewhere.

But she knew her son wasn't going to be happy leaving behind his new family. And Larissa could never live without her son.

"I don't want to live my mother's life, Jake," she said quietly.

"You don't have any family to disown you," he said.

Nice of him to point that out. She wrapped her arms around her waist and hugged tightly. "I have Peter."

"We have Peter," he said.

"We don't have anything except a media blitz between us."

He cursed under his breath. One of his less flattering habits was that tendency of his to curse when she made him mad. She made a mental note to lecture him on that at a later time.

He pulled the car to the side of the road and turned to face her. "I'm not sure what you want from me."

"Courtesy would be a nice start."

"I'm not being rude."

"Well, I don't understand these one-word answers."

"I can't be your best buddy, Larissa."

"Why not?"

"Because we're living together and I want that to be real. And you don't."

"It's not that I don't want it to be real."

"Then what is it?"

"What if I start believing this is real and you decide that I'm not the right woman for you to spend your life with."

"I'm not that flaky, Rissa. I know my mind."

"Right now you think you do because of Peter."

"Woman, are you trying to drive me insane?"

"No, I'm not. I just don't want to end up like my mom did."

"Alone?"

"Yeah, alone."

"Where was your dad?"

She took a deep breath and looked into Jake's eyes. There was no way she wanted to get into this conversation with him. But she wasn't prepared to spend the rest of her life or the rest of the weekend with Jake while he gave her the cold shoulder.

Taking a deep breath, she said, "I don't have one."

Eight

"No dad? I don't understand," Jake said. He rubbed the bridge of his nose with two fingers and tried to assemble everything she'd told him of her past. He knew she'd had a rough childhood and he didn't really want to be responsible for her having to relive it now. But he had to understand her.

He hadn't been able to sleep last night and his future evenings looked just as restless unless she gave up her idea of a platonic marriage. The only idea he'd had that might work was keeping a distance between them, but even that was next to impossible.

"Explain it to me," he said at last. She was seated next to him in a pretty pink dress that made her eyes seem even bluer. With her blond hair free around her shoulders she looked too feminine for him. Too soft and gentle and he was very afraid that his baser instincts would overwhelm him, despite his mother's best efforts to make him into a gentleman.

"There's not much to say. My mom trapped herself a husband, but Reilly wasn't interested in being a dad, so he refused to have any contact with me. When I was four, he ran off with his secretary, leaving us nothing."

"I'm sorry, Larissa. But I don't see how our marriage resembles your mom's. I've already told you I don't feel trapped. We were both there the night Peter was conceived."

She smiled at him—the first time she'd done so today, and though he knew he shouldn't let it, he felt that smile all the way to his soul. It made him feel bigger than he was—like a man who wasn't a disappointment to his dad. A man who hadn't spent most of his adult life dodging responsibility. A man who could be hers for the rest of his life.

"Thanks."

"You're welcome. Do you feel better now?" he asked.

She shrugged and glanced out the window of the car. Jake leaned back in the seat and thought about all Larissa had told him. He suspected she was leaving out some very important details. He realized suddenly that perhaps her own father's treatment of her had influenced her decision not to tell him about Peter.

"You kept Peter a secret because you thought I'd treat him the way your dad did you," he said.

She turned to look at him, but she didn't say anything. Her silence confirmed his suspicion. This was why he'd never dated a woman for too long. He knew he wasn't good at building relationships.

"I'd never hurt our son," he said at last. He meant it too. Realizing that made him doubt he should continue with his custody suit. Because the one thing that would really hurt Peter was not having Larissa in his life. And though he justified his suit as insurance that Larissa could never cut him out of their lives again, he knew it was more about payback. Suddenly payback didn't seem justifiable. He'd keep it on the back burner if this marriage didn't work out.

Larissa bit her lower lip, tears glittering in her eyes. "I know that. Believe me, Jake, I wouldn't have made love with you that night if I thought you were anything like Reilly was."

He should put the car back in gear and do what Nicola had suggested this morning before they left— pretend they were actors and show the world a couple in love. Jake knew he was going to have no problem pretending to be in lust with Larissa. His real problem was going to be remembering it was a charade.

"Then what did you mean by not wanting to end up like your mom?"

"Just that Reilly resented her."

"I don't resent you," he said, drawing his finger down the side of her neck. She shivered under his touch and leaned just the tiniest bit closer to him.

He leaned down and kissed the base of her neck. She trembled under his touch, her fingers coming to hold his head. He glanced up at her. Her eyes were closed and she held him with a fierceness he knew she'd deny.

They were both masters of hiding. But he didn't intend to let her hide anymore. She didn't want a platonic relationship with him and they both knew it.

He raked his teeth down the column of her neck and she moaned deep in her throat. He felt the vibrations against his lips.

"This is crazy," she said.

"This is right," he said, pulling her more fully into his arms. She wedged her hands between them and pushed away slightly.

"What now?"

"We said we'd try to keep this nonsexual."

"God, woman, how many times are you going to bring that up? I think it's obvious we're fighting a losing battle."

"I know."

"Then why'd you bring it up?"

She took a deep breath. "Because I'm not the type of woman who is going to make a good Danforth wife."

"Why not?"

"You need someone of your own class. Someone who comes from money and is used to eating on bone china and drinking from Waterford crystal glasses."

"I don't live like that."

"No, but your family does. And they're going to realize I'm not worthy of the Danforth name."

"I'm not sure I'm worthy of the name. But it's mine and once we're married it'll be yours. I don't want to hear any more about it from you."

"Yes, sir," she said.

"Woman," he growled at her.

She laughed. It made him feel lighter in that moment than he'd have thought possible. The more he learned of Larissa's childhood, the more he understood why she'd kept Peter a secret. Understanding wasn't the same as forgiving, though.

"Now, let's get back on the road. I don't want to miss our flight," he said, putting the car in gear.

"Want a drink?" Jake asked once they were seated on the plane in Atlanta. There hadn't been a direct flight to Vegas from Savannah.

"Yes, something strong."

"Still wigged out from the landing of our flight from Savannah?" he asked, waving the flight attendant over to them.

"I'd like to say no," she said.

He ordered two bottles of Corona. He handed her

one and Larissa played with the lime and bottle while other passengers filed past them, taking their seats.

"It felt like we were on a roller coaster. I hate roller coasters," she said.

"I love 'em," he said, tilting his bottle back and taking a long drag.

Was there a better example of all that was different between them? "You would. I'm not like that."

"Like what?"

She thought about it for a minute. "Adventurous."

"I'd disagree with that. In some settings you are extremely adventurous."

"Which ones?" she said.

He leaned closer to her. His spicy cologne surrounded her and then she felt his breath brush against her cheek. "Intimate ones."

She gave him a secret smile. Every time she was convinced they were an ill-suited match, this physical spark flamed back to life. There was a bond between them that went way beyond being parents to Peter, and touched on her secret fear of depending too strongly on this man.

"Drink your beer before I decide to test that adventurous spirit," he warned.

She took a sip of her beer and threw caution to the winds. "What if want to take that test?"

"You don't. Platonic friendship, remember?" he asked.

"Hoisted on my own petard," she said. She wondered if she'd merely issued Jake a challenge by insisting on a platonic marriage—a challenge he'd be helpless to resist. She knew him well enough to know he liked to win. Was that why she'd done it? So she could say he'd seduced her into changing her mind? So she could blame him if things went wrong?

She didn't dwell on that too closely, because it made her the worst kind of manipulator. She was only fooling herself. Jake wanted her and had made no bones about it. She was the one attempting to play it safe...and failing miserably.

"Indeed. Changed your mind?"

Time for honesty, Larissa. "About a dozen times but I always come back to the same decision."

"No sex?" He arched an eyebrow at her.

If she changed her mind it would make this ache deep inside her go away. For a little while, things would seem fine between them, but she suspected in the end she'd end up with a bigger ache. "Yes," she said quietly.

He finished off his beer. "In that case I'd better find something to distract me."

She took a sip of her beer and pulled the SkyMall catalogue from the pocket in front of her. Their time in the air passed quickly.

"The pilot has turned on the fasten-seat-belt sign signaling our descent into the McCarran International Airport."

Larissa nervously gripped her armrest. Once the

plane landed, everything would be out of her control. Jake had worked on his laptop through most of the flight. He'd scheduled a meeting for late this afternoon with the Vegas D&D's. She was a little in awe of his business persona. It was nothing like the frat boy she'd known in their college days or the man she'd come to know since Jasmine Carmody had forced them back into each other's lives.

He put his hand over hers on the armrest and pried her fingers free. "Nervous?"

"Yes."

"Don't be. I'm right here and I won't let anything happen to you," he promised. Lifting her hand to his lips, he brushed a soft kiss against her knuckles.

She bit her lip and looked away from him and out the window. That was the problem. Jake was here and she wanted to believe it was forever. It was getting harder and harder to remember that he was here because his family had forced him to marry her to save face.

He'd been solicitous during their flight—friendlier than he'd been in the car on their way to the airport. She'd been tempted to lift the armrest and scoot as close to him as she could, to rest her head on his shoulder while he worked. She wanted to pretend for a minute that they were really going to Vegas to marry because they couldn't bear not being man and wife any longer.

But she knew the truth and that knowledge had

kept the armrest firmly in place and her head on the back of the leather first-class seat.

He lifted the armrest and tugged her against his side. Leaning close to her, he whispered, "'The woods are lovely, dark and deep.'

She glanced up at him. God, this felt too right. Too good. But for this moment, while the plane was landing, she wasn't going to pull away. She was going to stay close to the only man she'd ever trusted and repeated the words of their poem to.

Together they recited the rest of Frost's poem. The last line echoed in her head…*miles to go before I sleep*. She'd felt alone on her journey for so long. But as she glanced up at Jake and saw him watching her with those brown eyes of his, she didn't feel alone anymore.

And in her heart she knew she'd never be the same. Because Jake wasn't just the right man to fix the mess Jasmine Carmody's report would create, he was the right man to fill the emptiness in her soul.

Every time he thought he had Larissa figured out, she did something that made him realize he didn't. He'd meant to keep his distance from her, but he'd been unable to. In all the years he'd known Larissa, he'd never realized how much of herself she kept from the world, and especially from him.

The one thing she'd never tried to hide was how much their son meant to her, and he had a few doubts about the wisdom of continuing with his plan to sue for full custody of Peter.

Larissa started to pull out of his arms when the plane pulled up to the gate. He stopped her with a quick kiss. She smiled up at him and he felt it in his groin. He didn't know if he could keep up the dual life that they'd decided on. Public touching and kissing, private hands-off.

Yet, she'd said again today she wasn't ready to make love with him. And he wasn't going to push her. He was going to sit back and let fate direct him. Hell, no, he wasn't. He was going to do his damnedest to make sure she came to the same conclusion he already had.

"Nicola has arranged for a reporter to meet us here."

"Jasmine Carmody?"

"No. Another one who will write up a piece about how in love we are and how circumstances kept us apart."

"What circumstances?" she asked.

"My traveling, your job. We'll be vague. The important thing is to appear totally in love."

"Totally?"

"Yes," he said. Nicola had said nothing about appearing to be in love, but Jake wanted to know what it would be like to have Larissa look at him with complete devotion.

"I'm not sure I can do this."

"Too late to back out," he said.

"I won't leave you hanging, Jake. That was just nerves."

"Would it be so hard to love me?" he asked.

She bit her lower lip and closed her eyes. They were so close she was still in his arms, but he felt a gulf open between them. He felt the space that Larissa used to protect herself from relationships open up. He felt her backing away and did the only thing he could think of to pull her back to him.

Storm her barricades. Lay siege to the fortress that was her body and win the battle. He brushed his lips back and forth over hers. "Don't fight it," he whispered.

"Fight what?" she asked, against his mouth.

"This," he said, angling his head and taking her mouth the way he wanted to take her body. With long thrusts of his tongue. Claiming every inch of her mouth with his own.

She opened for him and he felt her capitulation. This was the one place where they communicated with total honesty. Seducing her with tender pulls of her lips, he pushed his own hammering desires to the back burner and strove for patience.

He smoothed his hands down her back, bringing their chests together. Her heart hammered against his. She felt small and fragile in his arms.

Lord, she tasted better than he remembered. It felt like it had been years since he'd last held her like this. Then the dynamic of the kiss changed. Larissa lifted her hands to frame his face and tasted him with long, slow kisses.

Dammit, he was the one in control, he thought. But as she scraped the edges of her fingernails down the side of his neck, he gave up all pretense. He was putty in her hands.

Sliding his hands to her waist, he started to pull her onto his lap. He needed her over him now. He was hard and straining and he honestly didn't think he could wait another second to bury himself in her body.

"The captain has turned off the fasten-seat-belt sign, you are now free to gather your things and disembark."

Larissa jerked away from him. He cursed under his breath, dropping his head to his hands and breathing deeply to try to regain some control. He'd been ready to take her here in the damn airplane.

The other passengers began gathering their luggage and filling the aisle. There was no way he was going to be able to walk off the plane until he'd had a few minutes to forget about the incredible woman he'd just had in his lap.

He glanced over at her. She watched him with wide eyes that were full of confusion and possibly hope. She touched her lips gingerly.

"I'm not going to apologize," he said.

"Good. I'm not either."

He'd forgotten how sensual she was. Forgotten that night in Atlanta when he'd discovered that her passion for books and words extended to him as well. "I figured total lust would make better headlines than being in love."

"Good idea."

She gathered up her purse and unfastened her seat belt, preparing to stand. He put his hand on her arm, holding her in her seat.

"Aren't you ready to get off the plane?"

"No," he said.

She gave him a quizzical look. He gestured to his lap. Her eyes widened.

"I guess I do owe you an apology."

"Not on your life, Larissa."

She got that heavy-lidded look in her eyes and leaned toward him, but he held her back. "I'm an inch away from saying to hell with it and seeing if we can both squeeze in that rest room up there."

"Jake—"

He covered her lips with his fingers. "Not another word."

The last of the passengers filed by and Jake felt better under control. He picked up his briefcase and stood, keeping his hand on Larissa's elbow as they exited the plane.

She tugged her arm out from under his grip and took his hand. She slid her fingers through his. He glanced down at their joined hands and tried to not let it matter. Their holding hands shouldn't mean anything, but it did.

She trusted him. If she didn't want to admit that, it was fine with him. But he knew there was something between them now that hadn't been there before.

Nine

Larissa smoothed her hands down the sides of her simple wedding gown. She wasn't sure who had arranged for it, but there had been a small fortune in wedding gowns in the suite when Larissa had arrived. Jake had told her to pick one. He'd left her alone in the suite for the past four hours.

The hairdresser, makeup artist and photographer had arrived forty-five minutes ago and now she looked like someone she didn't recognize. Oh, God, what was she doing?

"Can I have a few minutes to myself?" she asked.

"Yes, ma'am." All three filed out of the room.

Larissa walked to the mirror staring at the woman

there. A woman who was sleek and sophisticated and not at all like the woman Larissa knew herself to be. She looked in the mirror like a woman suitable to be a Danforth wife.

She reached toward her reflection, touching the glass. This wasn't real. This was all pretend. Game face and all that.

But it felt real. It felt like the dreams she'd secretly harbored since she'd given birth to Peter. It's not real, she reminded herself again.

There was a rap on the door and Larissa went to answer it.

''Sorry, ma'am, but it's time to go upstairs for the ceremony.''

She nodded. The hairdresser took the veil from her hands and placed it on her head. Tears burned the back of her eyes. She was alone with strangers, people paid to help take care of her because she had no family of her own to help with these moments. No mother to help her with her veil. No sisters to help pick out flowers or choose bridesmaid dresses. Just her. Alone. The way she'd always been.

The chapel was small and intimate. Jake stood at the front, talking to the photographer and Artie O'Neil, the reporter that Nicola had arranged to have write about their wedding.

Larissa tried to smile. Tried to pretend that this was what she wanted. That she was marrying a man who loved her. But she felt sick.

She turned and blindly ran down the hall. She heard voices and someone calling her name, but she didn't stop. She escaped through the fire exit and paused on the stairs.

She leaned back against the wall and wrapped her arms around her waist. She was crying. Crying for things that she'd never had. Crying for the dream that now seemed so childish and ridiculous. Crying for something that she'd never realized she wanted until now.

The door opened and she felt raw, exposed.

"Rissa, what's wrong?" Jake asked softly.

She tried to swallow so she could speak, but she couldn't. She turned her head from him.

He closed the door and walked toward her. She put her hand up. "Don't."

He stopped and she tried to pull herself together. But her mind was filled with pictures of perfect families. The kind of family she'd been trying to create for Peter. What she wanted and what she would have were very different.

"Talk to me, baby. I don't know what you need."

She didn't, either, and that was the problem. How was she going to be able to explain that she wanted something she'd never had? That today, when she was standing at the back of the chapel, she realized she wanted a mother? A real mother who would have noticed her daughter and not stayed mired in her own bitterness.

"I...I'm sorry."

Jake closed the gap between them and pulled her into his arms. "About what?"

She shrugged. When he held her like this she didn't want to leave. She wanted to believe the illusion they were presenting to the world was true. "This. Being so emotional."

Jake tipped her chin back and she stared up at him through the filmy lace of her veil. "A wedding is a big deal in a woman's life."

"What about a man's?" she asked.

"What?"

"Is this a big deal to you, Jake?" She should have kept her mouth shut, shouldn't have worried about what he was going to say, but she did. She didn't want him to answer unless he said the words her wounded heart needed to hear.

He pushed her veil up and smoothed it back away from her face. Without the barrier between them, his breath brushed her cheek and his eyes were very sincere. He leaned close to her and whispered, "You're the only woman I've ever asked to marry me. You know this is a big deal."

She sighed. She did know that. Jake was a good man. A good man who she was falling more and more in love with each moment she spent with him.

She realized suddenly that her tears had nothing to do with the family she'd never really had and everything with wanting Jake to marry her for love and not convenience.

He handed her a snowy handkerchief that bore his monogram. She wiped her face and saw the residue of the makeup she wore on it.

"I just felt so alone," she said.

"Well, you're not. We're in this together."

"Sorry I made a mess of my makeup."

"I don't care about that."

"You don't?"

"Rissa, you're the most beautiful woman I've ever seen."

Suddenly things didn't seem quite as desperate as they had earlier. "Thank you."

"You're welcome. Are you ready to get married now?"

She nodded. He gently kissed her forehead and lowered her veil once again. Then taking her hand firmly in his, he led her back to the chapel. When they exchanged vows, a part of her began to believe that Jake never would leave her.

Larissa smiled for the pictures after their wedding, and even though Jake knew that they were playacting, it felt real to him. A little too real, he thought uncomfortably. He'd always been a loner even though he'd been surrounded by siblings and cousins. There'd been a core part of himself he'd kept private. Larissa was the only person he'd ever let get a glimpse of it.

And now they were married. Jake moved away to have a few final words with the reporter.

Larissa was standing by herself. She'd clung tightly to his hand throughout the ceremony and he remembered promising her he'd help shoulder her burdens. He knew she didn't believe his words. But when he'd looked into her eyes and given her his vow, he'd realized he meant them. Legally she was his and there was a sense of rightness that accompanied that feeling.

Artie promised to send a rough draft of the article to Nicola for approval before his magazine printed it. Soon they were alone. Just him and his bride. The primitive part of Jake's soul was ready to claim her. To throw her over his shoulder and carry her upstairs and push aside her doubts. To prove to her that she'd made the correct decision when she'd pledged her life to him.

But he'd been raised with more sophistication than that. He'd arranged for them to have dinner on the rooftop of the hotel. Away from the prying eyes of any reporters.

Away from the intimacy of their suite. He crossed the chapel to her side.

''What else do we have to do tonight?'' she asked nervously. He knew she hadn't liked the public part of their wedding—the pictures that would be sent to magazines and newspapers, the questions that Artie had asked and they'd answered.

"Nothing. The evening is ours."

She flushed a little and licked her lips. God, she was making all his good intentions hard to carry out.

"I've got a surprise for you."

"Really? What is it?" she asked, tilting her head to the side. He noticed she did that when she was in a contemplative mood. What was going on in her head?

He wished he understood her better. But he was honest enough to admit understanding Larissa or any woman had never been a top priority.

"A secret that I think you'll like. Now close your eyes and follow me."

"Okay."

He took her hand and led her to the elevator. He used the passkey he'd gotten from the casino manager to access the rooftop. When the doors opened, he pocketed the key and lifted Larissa into his arms. He walked to the table surrounded by candles and string lights. He set her on her feet.

"Open your eyes."

Larissa looked around at the romantic setting. A dining tent had been set up on the roof. It was draped in sheer gossamer fabric and lights twinkled from underneath it. She saw a table set for two. Beyond the dining area, the night sky was bright with the lights of the Vegas strip. But the smooth sounds of Jimmy Buffett poured from the speakers.

"Stars Fell on Alabama" was playing. It was their

song. The song they'd danced to at the reunion on the night they'd made love.

Jake led her under the canopy and they were secluded from the world. She felt that she was the wrong woman in the wrong place. This was a romantic dream and not at all anything that practical Larissa Nielsen had ever experienced. But she wasn't Larissa Nielsen anymore. She was Larissa Danforth. And maybe romance was what she needed.

"Dance?" he asked.

She nodded and he pulled her into his arms. Her head fell to his shoulder and he danced her around the rooftop. "It feels like a lifetime since that night," he said.

Jimmy Buffet sang…*did it really happen?* And it was a question that Jake had asked himself many times since he'd last made love to her. The memory of it was so vivid and so real, and yet unbelievable.

"I was so nervous about dancing with you," she confessed.

"Why?"

"Because you're a good dancer and I'm not."

"I didn't notice that."

"I didn't either. Once you took me in your arms, all my worries dropped away. It was…magical."

He didn't say anything, but he'd felt the same way. It had been a magical night. A moment out of time to be treasured for always. He lowered his head and dropped nibbling kiss down the side of her neck. She sighed and tipped her head to the side to give him greater access.

He sucked lightly at the pulse beating strongly at the base of her neck. She shivered in his arms. He soothed her with languid strokes of his hands down her back.

She pushed her fingers into his hair and pulled his head down to hers. Raising on tiptoe, she kissed him. Her lips moved over his with intent, arousing in him a need that had never been sated.

He wanted to let her take the lead so that later on there'd be no question of him seducing her. But he couldn't just stand there. He stopped dancing and lifted her in his arms with his hands on her buttocks and thrust his tongue deeply into her mouth.

He craved her. He doubted that anything less than total surrender would satisfy the ache that kept growing inside him.

She pulled back, gasping for breath and watching him with wide eyes. He dropped his hands and stepped away from her, clenching his fists at his side.

"Let's eat."

"Jake?"

"Not right now, Larissa. Food, first."

"I don't want food."

He paused and glanced over at her. "What do you want?"

"You," she said, and walked toward him purposefully.

* * *

Blood rushed through his veins, pooling in his groin as she walked closer. He staggered back and had to sit down on one of the dining chairs. He'd expected to have to woo her slowly. He had, in fact, arranged for total privacy for them on the rooftop by asking the hotel staff to wait for his request before coming upstairs.

She continued toward him, a smile spreading over her face. The music still played in the background— no longer Jimmy Buffett but some smooth-sounding classic jazz. Miles Davis. Not an artist that was his favorite but one that he knew Larissa loved.

She paused. "Miles Davis?"

He nodded.

"How'd you know?"

"Woman, you've got about fifteen different CDs of his."

"You're observant."

Only when something mattered, he thought. And Larissa mattered to him in ways he was only beginning to explore.

"I like that," she said, still moving toward him slowly.

"Good." He stood and crossed the small space between them in two strides. It had been an eternity since he'd last held her in his arms.

He'd been aroused since they'd stepped off the plane and no amount of work, exercise or cold showers had dulled it.

Her mouth opened under his and he told himself to take it slow, but slow wasn't in his programming with this woman. She was pure temptation. He slid his hands down her back, pulling the zipper of her dress down at the same time.

Her bodice loosened, and from his angle looking down at her, he could see the tops of her breasts and the barest hint of her nipples. He lowered his head, using his teeth to pull the loosened fabric away from her skin.

She wore a demure cotton bra under her wedding dress and that simple undergarment made something clench deep inside him. Her nipples stood out against the plain fabric. He ran the tip of one fingertip around her aroused flesh. She trembled in his arms.

He undid the front clasp of her bra and brushed the cups away. Lowering his head, he took one of her nipples in his mouth and suckled her. She gasped his name and held him to her with a strength that surprised him. He pulled back and blew lightly on her skin.

She shivered and tried to direct his attention to her other nipple, but he held back. Knowing that his control would shatter at any moment, he wanted to savor this feeling of anticipation while he still could.

Her other nipple pouted for his attention, growing harder under his stare. He lifted one hand to touch her and saw the differences between them. His hand was huge and her breast small, smooth…flawless.

He cupped her breast, rubbing her nipple with the palm of his hand. Rissa tilted her head back, her hands still clutching at his head. Her mouth opened and he heard her moan his name.

He took that other nipple in his mouth. Teased her with his tongue and then the edge of his teeth, scraping carefully against the nubby texture.

Her fingers drifted down his back and then slid around front to work on the buttons of his shirt. She took a half step back and pushed his shirt open. She growled deep in her throat and leaned forward to brush kisses against his chest.

He continued caressing her breasts until they were full and her nipples prominent. He slid his hands down her smooth skin. Everywhere he touched he wanted to linger, but tonight wasn't for extended love-making. They had been apart too long.

She bit and nibbled at his chest. His groin hardened so painfully, he could take his pulse between his legs. He felt like her plaything. He wanted to lie back and let her have her way with him. But there was no room here.

He pulled her to him and lifted her slightly so that her nipples brushed his chest. Holding her carefully, he rotated his shoulders and rubbed against her. Blood roared in his ear. He was so hard, so full that he needed to be inside of her body *now*.

Impatient with the yards of satin pooling at her hips and down to her toes, he shoved them up and out of his way. He caressed the long length of her thighs. She was so soft. She moaned as he neared her center and then sighed when he brushed his fingertips across the front of her panties.

The cotton was warm and wet. He slipped one finger under the material and hesitated for a second, looking down into her eyes.

Her eyes were lidded. She bit down on her lower lip and he felt the minute movements of her hips as she tried to move his touch where she needed it.

He was beyond teasing her or prolonging their torture. He pushed her panties aside and plunged two fingers into her humid body. She squirmed against him.

He lifted her and crossed to the table in two long strides. He sank to the chair and pulled Larissa over his lap.

He turned Larissa in his arms. "What are you doing?" she asked.

"Trust me," he said.

She murmured something he didn't catch.

"Rissa?"

"Yes, Jake. I trust you."

He guided her hands to his shoulders. "Hold on."

Reaching between their bodies he freed his erection and then pushed the satin of her skirt to her waist. He held her hips in his hands. She was soft and womanly. Their naked loins pressed together and he shook under the impact.

He had to have her. Now. She was naked to the waist and he used one hand to pluck at her aroused nipples, the other testing the readiness of her desire for him. He found her wet and ready. He adjusted his hold on her hips and then entered her with one long, hard stroke.

She moaned his name and her head fell forward, leaving the curve of her neck open and vulnerable to him. He bit softly at her neck and felt the reaction all the way to his toes when she squirmed in his arms and thrust her hips toward him.

A tingling started in the base of his spine and he knew his climax was close. But he wasn't going without Larissa. He wanted her with him. He caressed her stomach and her breasts. Whispered erotic words of praise and longing in her ears.

She moved more frantically in his arms and he thrust into her deeply with each stroke. Breathing through his mouth, he tried to hold back the inevitable. He slid one hand down her abdomen, through the slick folds of her sex, finding her center. He stroked the aroused flesh. She continued to writhe in his arms no closer to her climax than before.

He circled that aroused bit of flesh between her legs with his forefinger, then tickled it very carefully with his nail. She screamed his name and tightened around him. Jake pulled one hand from her body and locked his fingers on her hips, holding her still for his thrusts.

He penetrated her as deeply as he could. Suckling at the base of her neck, he came long and hard.

He held her carefully in his arms and cradled her to him.

This marriage that had started out as a media Band-Aid had just become very real. And Jake didn't know whether he liked that or not.

Ten

Aftershocks of pleasure still rocked her body. She closed her eyes and leaned fully into him. Jake held her with a strength that scared her. *What had she done?*

He was big and strong and more man than she'd ever known—the only man who'd ever seen the real Larissa and now she was his wife. And she wanted it to last forever. Not just until Abe Danforth won or lost his senate bid.

Forever…that elusive thing had always been just out of her grasp. She had Peter, but in her heart she knew one day he'd leave her as well. But Jake had never been hers and she had the feeling he never would need her as deeply as she needed him.

This couldn't happen again. And yet she didn't know if she'd be able to keep her hands to herself. One time wasn't enough. She still wanted him. She hadn't gotten to explore his body and relearn his shape. She doubted a lifetime would be long enough for that.

Her cheek rested on his shoulder and she never wanted to leave the circle of his arms. If only this moment could last forever.

"Well, Mrs. Danforth." Jake sounded much too pleased with himself.

He idly stroked her back and the hair on his chest tickled her nipples. She didn't want to want him again. She wanted him out of her system so she could move on with her life. A life that had been disrupted by him and the emotions he evoked in her.

"Well what?" she asked, lowering her head and nipping his pec. The muscle flexed under her mouth and she traced a random pattern with her tongue. He tasted good. Salty and masculine like only Jake did.

He cupped her jaw and tilted her face up to his. His nostrils flared with each breath he took and she knew he was reaching the point of no return. She was already there. Her center was dewy and her body ached to be taken by him again. To have him fill her until she couldn't think of anything but the pleasure he gave her.

She licked her lips, tasting him on her. He leaned

down and spoke directly into her ear. "That was a nice appetizer. But I'm hungry for more of you."

Her heartbeat sped up and everything feminine in her melted. The night breeze was cool and she shivered as it brushed over her aroused body.

Her mind said to step away from him but her body ignored that advice. This was her wedding night and likely the only one she'd ever have. She'd face the consequences of this night tomorrow.

She rubbed her nipples against his chest and tugged his head down to hers. His pupils dilated and his breath came in short pants. His erection pressed urgently against her and she doubted they were going to make it off the rooftop tonight.

He thrust against her and groaned as he encountered layers of skirt. "Damn. I want you naked."

"Me, too," she said, bathing his chest with kisses. She slid off his lap and lowered herself to her knees in front of the chair. She took his hard length in her hands.

He held himself still. His hands in her hair moved in circles and his hips thrust toward her the slightest bit. She knew what he wanted. What she wanted. Taking his buttocks in her hands, she drew him forward until the tip of him brushed her lips. She breathed against him and heard him groan.

She tasted him with delicate licks, then took the tip into her mouth. He shuddered. She felt his hands tighten in her hair and he pulled her to her feet. He fastened his pants with quick, careful movements, then refastened her dress.

"We need a bed. Now."

"Yes," she said. Her voice was husky and barely recognizable to her own ears.

Scooping her up in his arms, he carried her across the rooftop to the elevator. "There's a key car in my pants pocket."

She fished around for it, deliberately fondling him before she found the key. He staggered back against the wall and she knew she was playing with fire. He took her mouth in a kiss that demonstrated his dominance. It was deep and carnal and left her quivering in his arms. The elevator car opened and he carried her inside.

"Push the button," he ordered.

She did. The ride was mercifully short and soon they were in their suite. Jake carried her to the king-size bed and put her on her feet beside it.

His fingers made quick work of the zipper running down her back and her dress slid from her body, pooling at her feet in a sea of white satin. Jake stood there watching her. Her breasts were full and heavy, her nipples stood taut and ready for his touch. Her panties were long gone and her thigh-high hose were her only garments.

"Get on the bed," he said.

She stepped delicately out of her dress and turned slowly to crawl up the bed. She heard him growl deep in his throat and then felt his warm hand on her ankle. He tugged her flat.

"Don't move," he said.

She heard the sounds of him disrobing and then felt his naked body pressed along her back. She was completely surrounded by him. He held her like that for long minutes. His hands sweeping down her sides, his fingers reaching under her body to tweak her nipples.

He turned her over and sat back on his haunches watching her. He ran his forefinger down the center of her body. Helplessly she watched her sensitized skin grow rosy under his touch and when he skirted the curls at the apex of her thighs, she moaned softly.

He gave her a wicked smile but continued his path toward her feet. He reached her ankles and chained each one in his loose grasp. Then he slowly pushed her legs back toward her body. She felt totally exposed and vulnerable. And more turned-on than she'd ever remembered being.

He slid up her body, lowering his head he tasted her hot center with his lips and tongue. His hands left her ankles and he reached up to fondle both breasts.

He rubbed and pinched her nipples until her breasts felt too heavy, too full. She needed him. His mouth on her most feminine flesh was driving her toward orgasm, but she wanted Jake's body over hers. She wanted to watch his eyes as he took her and experienced a shared climax.

"Jake," she said, pulling on his hair.

"Come for me, Rissa."

"I want us to be together."

"We will…later. Please."

She couldn't deny him or her body. She rubbed her hands against his scalp and waited for his intimate touch. His breath brushed her first and then his tongue. His slid his hands down her body, gripping her hips and maneuvering her so that he had greater access to her secrets. He thrust one blunt finger into her channel and she clenched around it. He teased her with that one long finger, reaching up and pressing on a spot beneath her pubic bone. He continued to tickle the nubbin between her legs with his tongue and the twin pressures on her forced her over the edge. Her climax was intense and powerful but still she wanted more. She needed Jake.

He moved up over and held her still. He entered her with one long deep thrust. "Ah, that's it."

He penetrated her so deeply she felt they really were becoming one being. She lifted herself, tugged his head down to hers and took his mouth the way he took her body. He tore his mouth from hers as his thrusts increased. He lowered his head and suckled on one of her breasts and she felt a change come over him seconds before he flooded her with his release. Her own followed closely and she held him to her with a desperation she'd deny in the morning.

* * *

Jake ordered breakfast while Larissa showered the next morning. The night before had put to rest any doubts he had about making their marriage a real one. He wasn't sure what had changed her mind about keeping their marriage platonic, and frankly didn't care. He was starting to feel he and Larissa had a real chance at happiness, and that scared him.

But he was willing to do his duty this time. With a wry grin, he realized that duty had never felt so good. Slowly he was beginning to trust Larissa again. He understood now why she'd kept Peter a secret.

He picked up the phone and dialed Marcus's office. It was time to stop his bid to win full custody of Peter. Marcus had handed the paternity suit off to Ted Larson, one of his co-workers who specialized in family law. Jake got Ted's voice mail. He left his name and the number at the hotel for a return call.

The bathroom door opened and Larissa walked across the room to her suitcase. She wore a hotel bathrobe and a towel turbaned on her head. She looked cute and sexy at the same time.

"Come over here, woman," he said.

She gave him a haughty look over her shoulder. "You gave enough orders last night."

He had. And she'd responded to them beautifully. "I'm ready to take them," he said.

"I'll bet you are."

She rummaged through her clothes, selecting a

pretty sundress and undergarments. She headed back toward the bathroom with her clothes.

"Where are you going?" he asked.

"In there to change."

"You can change here. I'll be a good boy and keep my hands to myself."

"Well, that's kind of why I was going back in the bathroom."

"You don't want me to keep my hands to myself? No problem, Rissa." He stood up and walked toward her.

"Stop, Jake. I need to talk to you."

He didn't like the sound of that.

"About what?"

"Our intimate relations."

Sometimes you could tell Larissa was a librarian. "You mean our sex life."

"Yes. I think I gave you the wrong impression last night."

"No, you didn't, sweetheart," he said. Last night had been raw and earthy. He crossed to her and took her in his arms. "I still respect you."

"Oh, Jake. Not about that. I…I want to stick by our original agreement."

"Which one?" he asked.

She sighed and tilted her head to the side as she looked up at him. "The platonic one."

He cursed under his breath and stepped away from

her. The woman was trying to drive him insane. "Why?"

"Because sex makes things complicated. I'm sorry, I should have spoken up sooner, but I wanted a wedding night to remember."

"Good. I did, too. But this doesn't have to end."

"Yes it does."

"Explain it to me," he said.

"This wasn't real. The wedding, the setting, the dress. Everything was playacting."

"It felt real to me when I took those vows that made you my wife."

She blanched and looked away from him. "Me, too."

"Baby, I'm not like your dad. I'm not going to do to Peter what he did to you."

She wrapped her arms around her waist, holding herself so tightly that he knew he wasn't saying the right thing. Hell, he had no idea what the right words were. It was like being in virgin territory; he knew how to seduce Larissa into his bed, but he had no clue how to keep her there.

"I'm waiting to hear you say you know I won't hurt Peter."

"Of course I know that, Jake. The first time I saw you with him, I knew I'd cheated both of you out of something."

"Then what's the problem?"

"Me," she said, softly. "I'm the problem."

"You know I won't hurt you."

"What if I hurt you?"

"I'm not that fragile," he said. What kind of wimp did she think he was?

"That's what I was afraid of."

"I'm not following."

"I can't hurt you because I'm nothing more than a make-believe wife to you. You don't care for me."

"Don't put words in my mouth. I care for you more than I do any other woman."

"Right now."

"Larissa, there are no guarantees in life. You know that and so do I. I'm not sure what you think you're going to achieve by not sleeping with me."

"I'm trying to keep from falling in love with you, idiot. I don't want to be vulnerable to any man."

"I'm not just any man, Larissa. I'm your husband."

She shook her head and turned away. There was a knock on the door and Jake didn't move to answer it. He wanted to hash this out to a conclusion, but Larissa was already retreating behind that wall of icy cool that she used to keep him out. "Room service," they both heard from the door.

"This isn't over," he warned as he exited the bedroom.

Larissa was dressed by the time Jake returned. She'd clipped up her hair and was fastening her sandals when he walked back into the room.

"In a hurry?" he asked.

"No. I just didn't want…"

"To appear weak," he said. Cursing under his breath he stalked to his suitcase and removed his clothing for the day.

"Go eat, Larissa," he said without looking at her.

She stood in the doorway. "Didn't you want to finish our conversation?"

He gave a derisive snort. "No. I don't think so. I've had enough of trying to convince you I'm respectable." He walked away from her without a backward glance.

She shivered and rubbed her hands over her arms, feeling colder and more alone than ever. She'd expected Jake to say many things when she told him she wanted to stop sleeping with him. But she hadn't anticipated the depth of his anger.

She picked at the breakfast he'd ordered for them, but could only manage drinking the coffee. The phone rang and she answered it.

"Jacob Danforth please," a male voice said.

"One moment. Can I tell him who's calling?"

"Ted Larson."

Larissa set the handset on the table and crossed their suite to the bathroom door. The shower had stopped. She rapped on the door and Jake opened it, shaving cream on his face and a white towel slung low around his lean hips.

She swallowed. His hair was damp and a bead of

moisture trailed down his neck to his chest. Unconsciously she lifted her hand to catch the drop. Jake caught her hand in his and held her captive. She glanced up into his eyes.

She could read nothing in his gaze. Had she just made the biggest mistake of her life by demanding a celibate marriage with this man?

"Change your mind already?" he asked.

Sometimes it was as if he could see straight to her soul. Had she changed her mind? It would be so easy to loose herself in the web of sensuality that Jake created, but in the end, she knew she'd have a tough time moving on when he was tired of her. And Jake had never stayed with one woman too long.

She shook herself. "You have a call."

He rubbed her hand over his chest before letting it drop. She flexed her fingers, raking her nails over his skin. His towel stirred. She wanted to stay. What had she been thinking to put the brakes on this? "Take a message for me."

Her hand tingled and her body said her mind was on the verge of insanity. She couldn't live with Jake and not be his woman. "Okay."

She pivoted on her heel, but her legs were weak and she didn't know if she was going to be able to walk away from him.

"Rissa?"

She glanced over her shoulder at him. "Yes?"

"You never answered my question."

"I'm afraid to," she said, and walked away, firmly closing the bedroom door behind her. She needed to regain her perspective. She needed to talk to her son. She missed him. She'd talked to him right before the ceremony yesterday.

She took a message from Mr. Larson and left the note on Jake's briefcase. She dialed the number to Jake's parents' house. The housekeeper answered on the third ring.

"This is Larissa Nielsen...Danforth. May I speak to Peter?"

"Just a moment, ma'am."

"Hi, Mama."

Tears burned the back of her eyes. God, she missed him. They'd never been apart before this. "Hey, baby. I miss you."

"Me, too. I'm having so much fun here. I'm going to see some horses today."

Peter's happiness was palpable on the phone. Realizing she'd given her son something he never should have been denied made all the sacrifices worth it. She had to remember her marriage to Jake was for Peter. It wasn't for her and it certainly wasn't for Jake. "Good."

"When will you be home?" he asked.

Larissa wasn't sure of the exact time since Jake had their tickets but he'd said some time this evening. "Before bedtime."

"I love you, Mama."

"Love you too."

They said their goodbyes and she talked to Miranda briefly about what time to expect them. It felt weird to be discussing her son with someone else. She hung up and sat on the edge of the coffee table where she'd taken the call.

"You okay?" Jake asked from the doorway. He wore a pair of chinos and a shirt in a flattering shade of blue.

She nodded.

"Who was on the phone?"

"Ted Larson. I took his number for you. I called to check on Peter."

"How's he doing?"

"Great. They're going to see some horses today."

"That would be the stables near the house. Does he ride?"

"Jake, he's three."

"So?"

"No, he doesn't ride."

"We'll have to teach him," Jake said.

"Is this going to work?" she asked without thinking.

"Yes, Rissa, it is. I'm angry right now, but I'll get over it and we're going to work things out," he said, and there was a promise in his voice that she trusted.

"For Peter?"

Jake crossed the room to her side and tipped her head back with his knuckle under her chin. "For us."

Then he slipped away to make his phone call. She cautioned herself not to believe him but she couldn't help it. Hope had been born and she believed they had a chance at forever.

Eleven

"Oh, no," Larissa said as they pulled to a stop in front of his town house a little before ten that night. Peter was sleeping fitfully in the back seat and Larissa had been in a quiet mood since they'd left Vegas.

"What's the matter?"

"I recognize that car," she said.

Jake waited.

"It's Jasmine Carmody. What's she doing here?"

Jake reached over and patted Larissa's hand. "Probably checking up to see if our marriage is a real one."

"Let's go to my place. We can hide out until she leaves."

"I'm not hiding from anyone. Especially a reporter."

"I guess you're right."

"Of course, I am."

Jake pulled into the driveway and shut off the car. Larissa nervously twisted her fingers together. "Calm down. We're in this together."

He leaned across the seat and brushed his lips over hers. She sighed into his mouth and he hesitated, then deepened the kiss. He'd decided in the shower this morning to let Larissa set the pace for their marriage. She had too much sensuality in her to keep them apart for long. And once he'd gotten past his frustration, he'd realized she had a good point. Sex between the two of them was a convenient way to avoid talking.

Hell, he'd been the first one to use it that night in Atlanta when they'd conceived their son.

"Ready?"

"I guess."

"Chin up, Rissa. We're a team now and I don't think one determined reporter can defeat us."

She smiled at him and he felt ten feet tall. He climbed out of the truck.

"Mr. Danforth, I'm Jasmine Carmody with the *Savannah Morning News*. Can I have a few minutes of your time?" the stunning African-American woman asked.

"For what?"

"To discuss the circumstances of your recent marriage."

"What do you want to know?" Jake asked.

Larissa got out of the truck and walked around to his side. Jake pulled her close to his side and dropped a kiss on her forehead.

"Very touching," Jasmine said. "I'm curious about something."

"What's that?" Jake asked.

"How does it feel to know you're the second generation of wealthy Southern gentlemen to be deceived by a Nielsen woman?"

Larissa stiffened under his arm.

"I didn't deceive Jake."

"Of course, you didn't, Ms. Nielsen."

"It's Mrs. Danforth," Jake said. "And Larissa didn't trap me into marriage, Ms. Carmody. I trapped her."

"Do tell," Jasmine said.

"That's private and personal. I don't think we have anything further to say."

"I'm not giving up," Jasmine said. "I'm going to write this story with or without your cooperation."

"Then write this—Larissa and I have been friends for over ten years and our marriage has brought us the kind of happiness neither of us thought possible."

Jake lowered his head and kissed Larissa, hoping she'd understand from his embrace that he meant those words. Their marriage wasn't a temporary media fix, as it had started out—it was real and lasting. Because with Larissa, he'd found a place in his family. And a family of his own.

Peter stirred in the back seat of the car, coughing and crying out. Jake opened the back door and lifted out his son.

"Where's Mama?"

"Right here, sweetie," Larissa said, rubbing her hand over their son's head.

Peter squirmed in Jake's arms, leaning over toward Larissa. Jake let the boy go though he didn't want to. Peter coughed again and Larissa cradled him close to her.

"We better get him inside," Larissa said.

Jake closed the door and put his arm around Larissa. Jasmine continued to watch them and Jake had the feeling that they hadn't seen the last of her. But it didn't change the way he felt. He wasn't going to let a reporter hurt Larissa. She'd carved out a life for herself the only way she knew how.

"I didn't think she'd find out about your dad."

"Reilly Peyton isn't my dad. He was a sperm donor."

Jake laughed. She didn't sound angry with Jasmine. "You're okay that she found out."

"I'd rather she hadn't. But when you came to my defense I realized something."

Peter coughed again and Larissa rubbed his back. "I hope he's not getting sick."

"I'll call the doctor when we get inside," Jake said. He knew he should focus on Peter, but in the back of his mind her words lingered. "What'd you realize?"

"That having you by my side made all the difference in the world. Even if she prints her article—and I'm sure she will—it won't be me standing in front of Savannah society by myself. We're a family and together we'll decide what makes us Danforths. I've never really felt like I could fit in at home, either."

"Why not?"

"My father put a lot of pressure on me to be the responsible one. That eldest sibling thing, I guess. I've dropped the ball a lot, Rissa. You know I'm not perfect, but I'm not going to drop the ball this time."

"I know, Jake," she said. She reached up to touch him with her free hand.

"Let's get this little guy into his pajamas and then finish this conversation," Jake said.

"Mama?" Peter said, his breath rasping in and out. His chest was heaving with the effort to breathe.

Jake didn't like it. "Has he done that before?"

"No. Call the doctor," Larissa said. Though she tried to keep her voice calm, he saw her hands tremble.

Jake grabbed one of Larissa's laminated index cards and dialed the doctor's number. Larissa sat on the couch holding their son close and murmuring softly to him. But Peter kept struggling to breathe and

Larissa finally stood up. She paced around the room with their son in her arms. Jake was suddenly afraid that now that he'd found the happiness he'd always sought, he wouldn't be allowed to keep it.

Jake got the doctor on the phone and described Peter's symptoms. Dr. Gold instructed Jake to take Peter to the hospital, saying he thought Peter might be having an acute asthma attack.

Jake got his family out of the house and into the car, his heart pounding as he raced to the hospital.

Larissa had never been so scared in her entire life. Peter was hooked up to a drip IV and a nebulizer. His entire chest heaved with each breath he tried to take.

She clung tight to her son's hand and willed him to breathe easier, but she knew that wasn't possible. Jake rested his big strong hand on her shoulder, and she sensed he was urging her to share her burden with him but she couldn't.

She wouldn't be able to relax until Peter was off this machine and breathing easier, though she appreciated having Jake and his family around her. And she knew that Peter did as well.

Tonight she'd had her first taste of what being a Danforth meant. Instead of sitting in the waiting area until it was their turn, they'd been given a private room and admitted with little trouble. Dr. Gold had seen Peter once and this was the second breathing treatment that Peter had taken.

Jake's parents had arrived and were now in the waiting area. Jake hadn't left her side the entire time. He held her hand or Peter's and made sure they were very aware of his presence.

He was a solid support for Larissa and she realized she loved him. Watching him talk quietly to their son, and handle every detail that came up in the hospital had shown her what she'd secretly been afraid to admit all along.

Jake wasn't just her husband, he was her love. She also realized, when he'd talked to his family, that Jake kept the depth of his feelings a secret. It was humbling to know she might be the only one who realized Jake was so much more than the easygoing, successful businessman that he presented to the world.

Peter finished his breathing treatment and lay back against the pillows. He looked so small. Jake tucked Mr. Bear and Peter's worn blanket up next to him. Larissa leaned down and kissed him.

"Mama? Can we say our poem?"

"We sure can, baby."

Quietly she started Frost's poem and Jake and Peter joined in. By the time they'd gotten to the last line, Peter's eyes drifted close.

Larissa turned to Jake. "I feel so helpless."

"Me too."

She felt like crying. When she'd made her decision

not to tell Jake about Peter, she'd only had Reilly Peyton as an example—a man who'd never wanted to be a father. But from the first moment Jake had known about Peter, he'd proved that fatherhood was a natural part of him.

"Why are you looking at me like that?" Jake asked.

She didn't want to let him know how desperately she was coming to need him. "Like what?"

He shrugged and looked uncomfortable. "I'm not sure."

She slid off the bed and sat on his lap. Wrapping her arms around him, she held him tightly to her. God, she didn't think she'd survive if he left her.

"Thank you," she said against his lips.

"For what?" he asked, running his hands down her back and hugging her to him.

He smelled good. His cologne was spicy and woodsy, a direct contrast to the sterile scent of the hospital. "For being here. I'm so glad I didn't have to deal with this on my own."

He looked at her. His brown eyes were serious and she remembered all the promises he'd made her. Promises that she'd been afraid to believe. "That's my job now."

"Are you sure?" she asked, still afraid to accept his words.

He squeezed her tight and then tucked her head

under his chin. "Hell, yes. I'm not letting either of you out of my sight."

"Oh, Jake."

Jake kissed her with a passion that she sensed concealed hidden depths. She clung to him. For the first time in her life she really needed someone by her side and it scared her. Almost as much as her fear of being left alone. She watched Peter sleeping. Each exhalation wheezed a little.

Someone cleared their throat and she glanced up to see Harold Danforth in the doorway. Jake's dad was dressed in chinos and a button-down shirt. He looked tired and tense but his face filled with love when he glanced at his sleeping grandson.

"No need to ask how things are in here," Harold said.

Jake stiffened under her. Larissa got to her feet and walked over to the hospital bed to check Peter. She rested her hand lightly on his chest to feel each breath he took. "You know me, Dad. Can't keep my hands off a pretty girl."

"I do know you, son," Harold said. There was a pride in his eyes that Larissa realized Jake didn't see.

"Your mom and I wanted to check on Peter before we went home for the night."

"He's sleeping," Jake said.

"I'll go get your mother," Harold said.

Jake cursed under his breath and pushed to his feet, joining Larissa by Peter's side. Jake settled his hand over hers on their son's chest. "God, I hope he beats this thing."

"Dr. Gold said there's a chance he could outgrow the asthma."

Jake said nothing, but Larissa felt some of her anxiety wane. She knew that with Jake by her side there was nothing they couldn't handle.

"What's up with you and your dad?"

"Nothing," Jake said, pacing across the room.

"Jake?" She turned to face him, but he wasn't paying the least bit of attention to her.

"Leave it be, Rissa."

She crossed the room to Jake and wrapped her arms around him.

"Talk to me," she said at last. She'd been so caught up in her own feelings of inadequacy that she hadn't noticed the tension between Jake and his father before.

"I don't want to get into that. You've got enough on your mind with Peter."

She tilted her head back and met his eyes. "Peter's resting now. Tell me about your dad."

"It's nothing," he said, moving away. It seemed he couldn't stand still. "I've never been able to please the old man."

She stopped his pacing with a hand on his arm. "I don't get that from him. He seems really proud of you." That was the truth. Harold had taken her aside earlier and told her when the chips were down there was no better man to have by her side than Jake.

"Yeah, right. What dad wouldn't be proud of a son who can't keep his hands off his wife while his grandson struggles to breathe?"

"I'm sure your dad understands that we need each other now."

Jake shrugged.

Larissa wasn't sure what else to say. She thought Harold was probably relieved that their marriage wasn't just for the media, but she didn't want to open that topic of conversation. "It wasn't like that. And I think your dad knows it. You should talk to him."

"I don't think so."

She raised herself on tiptoe so they were almost eye-to-eye. "Well, I do. I think you should do it. And I'm not going to stop bringing the subject up until you do."

"We've only been married two days and already you're nagging me."

For the first time since they arrived at the hospital she felt like smiling. "Start out as you mean to go on, I always say."

"Good thing I know how to keep you quiet."

"How?" she asked, smiling teasingly up at him.

"Like this," he said, lowering his head and taking her mouth in a kiss that said things he'd never say with words. That embrace said thank-you and I'll be there for you. She clung to his broad shoulders and kissed him with the same intensity.

When his parents returned to the room, he reluctantly let Larissa go. A storm raged inside him. He'd never felt so helpless as he had on the drive to the hospital. He was used to focusing on a goal and achieving it. And tonight had shown him that life with Larissa and Peter was going to be anything but predictable.

Since they'd landed back in Savannah, he'd realized that the only thing he wanted was some peace and quiet with his small family. He wanted what his folks had always had, but he didn't know that he was worthy of that kind of bond. He'd played around with women for so long that, even though Larissa made him feel things that he'd never experienced before, he wasn't sure he could be the kind of man she needed.

She moved across the room toward his mother and Jake wondered how Larissa felt about suddenly having an extended family. He wouldn't give up being a Danforth for anything, he realized.

"How's Peter doing?" his mom asked.

"Better. He's finally sleeping," Larissa said.

"I hope this attack wasn't brought on by anything at our house."

"I'm sure it wasn't, Miranda. He had a great time visiting with you."

"We enjoyed having him there. God, I miss having a little boy in the house."

Jake loved his parents, but he wanted them to go so he could hold Larissa in his lap again and keep an eye on both her and Peter. "It's been a long night."

"Yes, it has," his dad said.

"I'm thirsty, I think I'll go down to the vending machine and get a Diet Coke. Want to go with me, Miranda?" Larissa asked.

"Sure, dear. Do you want anything, Jake?"

"Coke would be great, Mom."

Larissa followed Miranda toward the door. At the entrance, she paused and looked at Jake. *Talk to your dad,* she mouthed. Bossy woman, he thought as she disappeared.

His father leaned over Peter, brushing back his hair. "He looks so much like you."

Jake crossed to the other side of the bed and leaned down over his son. "Yeah, he does."

"This takes me back. Remember that summer you broke your arm?"

"Do I. I couldn't play soccer for six weeks."

"That's right. You missed out on winning that MVP trophy you'd had your eye on."

"I got it the next year."

"You were always good at winning."

"Yes, I was."

"You okay, son?"

Jake shrugged. It didn't matter that he was over

thirty and owned a successful business. He still felt like a boy in his dad's presence. His father was a man who had it all and made it look easy. Not even the disappearance of his youngest sister, Victoria, had phased Harold. He'd still held the family together and kept everyone focused on finding her. Jake didn't think he'd ever be the man his father was.

"Having a kid is a double-edged sword," his dad said suddenly.

"What do you mean?"

"Just that you do your damnedest to protect them and then out of the blue something you can't control happens." His dad reached out and touched Peter's forehead. In that moment he saw on his father's face the same vulnerability that Jake felt toward his son.

"Like with Victoria," Jake said. He'd never really gotten over the guilt he'd felt at her disappearance. And he'd never shared with his dad the responsibility he bore toward the incident.

"Yes," his dad said, running his hands through his hair. "Good news on that front. The body in the attic at Crofthaven isn't hers."

Jake felt a sense of relief at the news. No one in the family had given any credence to the theory that the body had been Victoria's. They all knew she'd disappeared in Atlanta, not in Savannah. "I never believed it was."

"Me either. God, I wish I knew where she was," Harold said. Another crack appeared in Jake's image of his dad. His old man had always appeared so capable and confident. Jake hadn't realized that underneath was a man who had as many vulnerabilities as Jake had.

"Me too. You know I've never forgiven myself for not attending the concert with her. I shouldn't have bought her those tickets."

His dad gave him a sad smile. "You never could tell her no."

That was the truth. He'd loved having younger sisters who looked up to him. Jake had always been indulgent with the women in his life. "It scares me sometimes to think that I might screw up with Peter that way."

"I wish I could tell you it ends, son."

"It doesn't?"

"No."

"How do you do it, Dad?"

"I lean on your mom. That woman is the best thing that ever happened to me. And you kids…well you're extensions of her."

Jake looked at his dad and for once didn't feel like a failure. "I hope I'm half the dad you are."

"I know you will be."

Before he could respond, the women returned with some cold soft drinks and a couple of bags of snacks.

"How's Peter?" Larissa asked.

"Still sleeping," Jake said.

Larissa crossed to his side and slipped her arm

around his waist. He held her close and watched their son sleep. A moment later, he glanced across the bed at his dad.

His dad winked at him and for the first time, Jake felt like a man that his dad was proud to know.

Twelve

The next evening Peter was doing much better, but Dr. Gold wanted to keep him one more night for observation. Larissa was tired—she hadn't slept in more than twenty-four hours. She was emotionally drained. Jake's family was wonderful, but they could be a little overwhelming. Jake's sister Imogene had breezed in on her lunch break wearing a power suit and looking totally gorgeous. Larissa had felt unkempt and frumpy by comparison.

Though obviously a workaholic, Imogene had spent part of her lunch break sitting at Peter's side and reading to him. Jake's brother Toby had called and Peter had talked to him on the phone. Wes had stopped by with a new electronic game for Peter, and all and all her son had seemed as overwhelmed as she'd felt at having so many people care about them.

But they were alone now. Jake was outside talking with his dad. She wasn't sure what had happened last night, but she felt like all the superficial reasons she'd been using for keeping Jake at arm's length had disappeared. She wasn't protecting her heart, because it was too late to do so. She'd fallen in love with Jake a long time ago and now that they were married she couldn't stop her feelings from deepening.

Peter had wanted her to sleep next to him, so she'd crawled into the bed with her son. Peter slept quietly, resting his head on her arm. She bent close and listened to his breathing. It was deep and steady. Relief flooded her and she hugged his small body close.

"Hey, lady," Jake said from the doorway. "How's our boy doing?"

She glanced up at him and felt her heart jump in her chest. Damn he looked good. Tired but good. He had two days' worth of beard stubble on his cheeks and he'd never looked more attractive. Sensual awareness flooded her body. Not now, she thought—I'm doing the mom thing.

"He's resting now. We were watching SpongeBob before he fell asleep. A show that Peter informed me you said he could watch. Correct me if I'm wrong but SpongeBob wasn't on my index card of approved television shows."

"Really? I'm sure I saw it on there," Jake said with a sly grin.

Peter loved having a daddy and it was just as clear that Jake loved being one. Jake had spent just as much time as she had at the hospital. He'd played games with their son and made plans to go camping this weekend down in St. Augustine. Listening and watching the two of them had convinced Larissa that Jake was in their lives for good.

"I'm going to let it slide this time, but once he's out of the hospital we'll go back to our normal TV schedule."

"Whatever you say, Larissa," he said in the bland tone that told her he was going to do whatever he thought was best for their son. She had to admit Peter had bloomed since Jake had come into his life. Her little boy had always been quiet and reserved. But lately he'd come out of his shell.

"Why do I get the feeling you're placating me?" she asked.

He shrugged, but there was a sparkle in his eyes that told her he liked sparring with her. "I don't know. You always were a smart woman—you tell me."

She prided herself on her intelligence, which made it even harder to believe that she'd actually thought she could live with Jake and not be his lover. Now she just had to figure out a way to bring the topic up so he'd know she'd changed her mind.

"Did your parents go home?"

"Yes. Mom said they'll be back in the morning when Peter is released."

Jake stopped at the side of the bed and ran his fingertip down her bare arm. She must look a mess. She reached up to tuck a strand of hair behind her ear but Jake brushed her hand away. "Leave it alone. I like it when you don't look all tidy."

"It's safe to say I'm not tidy at this moment." She carefully pulled her arm out from under Peter's head and stood up. Jake didn't back up and they were pressed almost body to body.

"No, you're not."

"Neither are you," she said, running her hands over his rough jaw. He felt earthy against her soft fingers and she wished they were alone. She leaned up and kissed him. Jake responded with a longing that took her by surprise. The kiss was carnal and deep and when he stepped away she shivered with desire.

"Rissa, is there something you're trying to tell me here?" he asked.

"Well, maybe I am."

"I'm not going to make any more guesses where you're concerned any longer."

"I'm sorry about that last morning in Vegas. I guess I freaked out."

"Our wedding night was incredible."

"Yes, it was. I don't want that to be our only night together."

"It won't be."

"Good, then we're on the same page."

"Larissa, we're not in a meeting with the library board."

She flushed. "I know. But it's easier to talk about it in business terms."

He shook his head. "Are you saying you want to be my wife, in every sense?"

"Yes," she said softly and cuddled closer to the man she'd given her heart to.

Jake felt he'd been through the ringer. He was used to blithely skating through life. Keeping his emotions in a nice safe place that was only breached by his siblings, parents and cousins. Over the past twenty-four hours he'd come to realize that Peter and Larissa had found their way into his heart.

Peter was naturally easy to love. The boy was a blend of Jake's rambunctious go-get-'em attitude and Larissa's quiet intelligence. It was an odd combination and it awed Jake to think that part of him was going to live on through Peter after he was gone.

And he'd realized he didn't want to lose this family he'd found, the family he'd created when he was still so self-involved that he'd never noticed. The family that he knew he'd never be able to survive without.

Larissa yawned behind her hand and her shoulder slumped with fatigue. She looked as if she was about to collapse. "Why don't you take the Suburban and go home and rest?"

He liked to think that he'd helped her through this crisis. And it had been a crisis. He could handle any major problem at D&D's, but nothing had made him sweat like watching Peter struggle to breathe. It had made him realize how fragile this life was. It had reminded him of all the reasons he'd started hiding his feelings when Vicky had disappeared. Only now he knew that hiding wasn't the solution. Celebrating life and remembering the reasons why it was good were important.

"Thanks, but I think I'd better stay here in case Peter wakes up."

"Don't you trust me to take care of him?" he asked. He had to wonder. She'd scarcely left him alone with Peter since they'd been at the hospital. Her quiet strength surprised him, but it shouldn't have. Larissa was a survivor.

She closed her eyes, hiding from him. As always, she was a mystery to him.

"Of course, I do. It's just I don't…"

"You don't what?" He wondered sometimes what she saw in him. She'd always been the one person that had slipped past his guard. The one person he could tell his dreams to who didn't make him feel like an idiot. The one person he'd always wanted to impress. And he had the feeling that sometimes he came close to doing that.

"I don't want him to need someone else," she said in a rush of honesty.

He understood. Sometimes it was easier to be everything to someone than to share the responsibility. "I'm not some stranger, Rissa. I'm his dad."

"You're right. I'm still not used to trusting men in general."

"Me in particular?" he asked. Hell, he sounded like a sap. Why did it matter if she didn't trust him? Because you love her, a voice inside him said. The thought staggered him.

She pivoted to face him. He couldn't read her expression, but he didn't care anymore. Now he was concerned with hiding his own weakness from her. He'd always been the strong one and he wasn't going to let anything—not even Larissa—change that. "I trust you, Jacob Danforth, more than I'd ever thought I could trust any man."

Her words went straight through him. The mantle of responsibility felt heavy on his shoulders and he vowed that he'd never do anything to make her doubt the faith she'd placed in him. God, he needed to be alone with his wife. He needed to know that his son was safe and healthy and then take his wife to bed and reaffirm the bonds they'd tentatively forged in Vegas.

"Come here, woman," he said.

"Why?"

Because I need you, he thought but didn't dare say. "Just get over here."

She gave him a flirty smile and walked across the room with slow hip-swaying steps. Each move she made seduced him. And made the barriers he'd thought he'd built around his heart crumble.

She stopped a good six inches from him. Her gaze skimmed over his body and he couldn't help it, he stood up straighter and flexed his muscles.

"Very impressive," she said.

"I know."

She laughed and he realized it had been too long since he'd seen Larissa smiling. He promised himself that from now on she'd have lots of reasons to smile.

He reached out and dragged her close. He wanted to clutch her to his chest but forced himself to just hold her loosely instead, carefully so not to reveal the intensity of the emotions swamping him. But deep inside he knew he'd never be complete without Larissa by his side. She made him a better man and he knew that if she ever left he'd be incomplete. How was he going to keep her by his side without letting her know?

Larissa left Jake and Peter at the hospital. She felt more certain than ever that she and Jake were going to make it. That they were going to be one of those couples that succeeded despite the circumstances under which they'd started their marriage. She returned to Jake's town house on autopilot and when she entered the house she went straight to his bedroom and crawled into his bed.

Surrounded by his scent, she fell into a deep sleep. The doorbell woke her four hours later. She stumbled from the bed and shrugged into Jake's robe.

She hoped it wasn't Jasmine Carmody again. Though she'd made a kind of peace with her past, that didn't mean she wanted to discuss it with that reporter.

A quick peak through the peephole showed that it was a man she didn't recognize. She opened the door.

"Can I help you?"

"Are you Larissa Nielsen?"

"I used to be. I'm Larissa Danforth, now." God that sounded right to her ears. She'd feared marrying into a moneyed family but she realized her fears were based on her father's attitude and her mother's marriage. Jake was so different than Reilly Peyton.

He handed her an envelope and walked away. She closed the door and reentered Jake's town house. That was strange, she thought. She went into the kitchen and put a cup of water in the microwave. She used her fingernail to open the envelope and pulled out the papers.

She skimmed them and lost feeling in her legs. Clutching the papers, she sank to the floor. Jake was suing her for full custody of Peter. He'd lied about the paternity test! He'd had it done so that he could take her baby away from her.

She pulled her knees to her chest and hugged them tight, realizing that her worst fears had been realized. She'd trusted him. And he'd betrayed her. The entire time he'd been playing a game calculated to hurt her in the worst way possible.

She staggered to her feet and went into the guest bedroom Jake had given her when they'd moved in. She took a shower and dressed with care. She didn't know what to do next but knew that she had to confront Jake. If he thought she was going to give up her son because he needed revenge on her, he had another think coming.

But she knew she'd never drag Peter through any kind of custody battle. She never wanted her son to feel as if his birth was something that brought regret to his mother and father.

When she was dressed, she got in her car and sat in the driveway while her hands stopped shaking. She leaned down on the steering wheel and tried to figure out how things could go from being close to perfect to a nightmare.

Finally she had her trembling under control and a slow anger began to build inside her. By the time she got to the hospital, she was ready to tear Jake Danforth apart. How dare he manipulate her that way? Didn't family mean anything to him? Didn't he realize how legal battles tore at a child's security?

She entered the hospital and rehearsed her words in the elevator on the way up. Then she thought about Jake's parents. Miranda had invited Larissa to call her Mom. Had she known that her son was planning to take Peter away? Had they all been in on the scheme to keep her from her son?

The elevator doors opened on Peter's floor and suddenly she was afraid to face the future. She knew that she wasn't going to be her usual levelheaded self. She knew that she was an inch away from tears and outright wailing.

She got off the elevator and walked slowly past the nurses station. It was early in the morning and the halls were filled with doctors making their rounds. She paused outside the door to Peter's room. Tucking a strand of loose hair back into her ponytail, she cautioned herself not to get emotional.

She pushed open the door and stepped inside. The room was dark except for a stream of sunlight coming through the gap in the curtains. Jake lay on the bed next to Peter. He cradled their son against his chest.

The scene looked so right. Too right. Maybe she should do the adult thing and back away. Let Jake have Peter. Jake could give him so many things that Larissa couldn't. He had a large family, plenty of money and most importantly, he loved Peter.

Tears burned the back of her eyes and she fought to keep them from falling but couldn't. They were hot on her face and when she lifted her clammy hands to wipe them away she caught a glimpse of her wedding ring.

She felt like a fool for ever believing that Jake would have wanted her for his wife. Maybe he'd just wanted to get her out of town so that he could build his case against her.

And she'd made it so easy by falling for him. By letting him manipulate her in the most intimate way.

A sob escaped her and she knew she wasn't in any shape to confront Jake right now. She turned to leave the room. She'd wash her face and get herself together.

"Rissa?" he asked.

She steeled her heart against the compassion she heard in his voice. Before, her lonely heart had been looking for love, but now she knew the truth. Jake was using his silky words and smooth ways to lull her into complacency. She glanced over her shoulder at him. Jake sat up, easing his arm out from beneath Peter and crossing the room to her.

"Baby, what's wrong?"

"I…" She couldn't get the words out of her mouth. How could she verbalize the hurt that had come on so unexpectedly? This was her worst fear and why she'd fought so hard to keep from falling in love with Jake.

"Did that reporter bother you again? I'm going to call my lawyers and have them take action against her."

Strangely those words were the ones that made her stop crying. "Call your lawyers?"

"Yes, my lawyers."

"You're good at that, aren't you?"

"What do you mean?" he asked, his eyes narrowing.

"That I'm well aware of how you've been keeping your lawyers busy—planning to take Peter from me."

Jake cursed savagely under his breath and Larissa took a few steps from him. Crossing her arms over her chest, she looked at him the way she would an enemy.

"Larissa—"

"Don't bother lying to me now, Jake. I've got the proof in my hands."

Jake shoved his fingers through his hair. A million excuses and defenses hovered on the edge of his tongue. He knew what to say and how to dance away from her. How to keep himself emotionally safe and protected from the vulnerabilities that only this woman could make him feel.

But seeing her hurting like this, knowing he was responsible, made him feel horrible. He didn't want to see her cry.

He pulled her into his arms. She struggled against him and he knew he only had a few seconds to say the right words. But what were they?

He caught her face in his hands and stared down

at her. He rubbed the tears from her eyes and leaned close to her. God, she was so small and vulnerable. "I'm sorry."

She started to speak, but he pressed his mouth to hers, stopping her words. She smelled so good and he knew he should be concentrating on making his mistakes right. She kept her mouth tightly closed but stopped struggling to get away from him. He lifted his head.

"I was angry when you first told me about Peter."

"I know. But I thought we'd gotten past all that. Dammit, Jake. I thought we were starting a life together."

"We are, Rissa. We have started a life together." He was hedging and she knew it. But if he told her what was in his heart and she didn't return his feelings, he'd feel like a fool. Better a strong man than a fool, he thought.

"It doesn't feel like this is much of a life. I wanted a real marriage, not one based on vengeance."

"I wanted revenge," he said honestly.

"I can't let you take Peter. You can offer him much more than I can when it comes to money and family, but you can't offer him the one thing that every child needs—love and nurturing."

"What makes you so sure?" he asked.

"Because you don't know how to love."

He shuddered. Jake shoved his hands through his hair and turned away from her. Was she right? Had he forgotten all he'd learned about loving relationships in trying to keep himself insulated from the pain that came with failing? He paced to the window and rested his head against the cold glass. There were no answers in the sky or in the densely crowded parking lot below.

The only place with the answers was inside him. And losing Peter or Larissa wasn't an option. He needed them in his life.

He straightened and turned back to the woman who didn't realize she held his heart in her hands. She watched him carefully, clearly not sure what to expect next. He realized it was time to stop running and stop hiding from the emotions that scared him the most and the woman who inspired them.

"I'm not going to take Peter away from you. Hell, woman, I don't think I could live without the both of you in my life. And I certainly can't live with the knowledge that I hurt you so deeply."

"I never could have gone through with the suit. It was my back-up plan. A safe way for me to pretend I could keep you under my control."

He opened his arms and she hesitated only a second before running across the room and jumping into his arms. He held her tight and whispered all the words he was afraid to say out loud.

"You are the breath in my body, the light in my soul and the beating of my heart. I can't survive without you. I love you."

"Oh, Jake. I love you, too."

He bent to capture her lips with his and this time she opened her mouth to his. The kiss was deep and sensual, but heavy with the promise of tomorrow. A promise Jake hadn't been able to believe in for a long time.

"Mama? Daddy?" Peter called from the bed.

Jake pocketed the legal papers Larissa had brought with her and they crossed the room to their son.

"Hey, baby. How do you feel?" Larissa asked, brushing his hair back from his forehead.

"Hungry," Peter said.

Jake laughed. His son was always hungry. "I'll go get you some food. What do you want?"

"Krispy Kremes."

"Peter, how do you know about doughnuts?" Larissa asked.

"Daddy told me about them last night and promised we could go as soon as I leave the hospital."

"Sounds like a good plan," Larissa said.

The doctor entered the room and in a short while Peter was discharged. Jake's parents arrived and Jake felt really worthy of being a Danforth for the first time since Victoria had disappeared. He realized that his coffeehouse business and his playboy lifestyle were just excuses to keep from staying still long enough to feel the guilt.

But he let go of the guilt. He knew his sister was

alive somewhere and he knew that they would find her.

"Mom and Dad, will you take Peter in your car? We're going to the Krispy Kreme."

"Sure thing, son," his dad said.

Jake took Larissa's hand in his and led her to the Suburban. "What are we doing?"

"I just wanted a few minutes alone with you, Rissa."

"I thought we settled everything."

"I'm going to call Ted Larson as soon as his office opens and drop the custody suit."

"I know."

"You sound pretty confident," he said.

"Honey, you told me I was the air you breathe. I think that gives me the right."

"Am I the air you breathe?"

She leaned up and kissed his jaw. "No."

"No?"

"You're the blood in my veins."

He scooped her up in the parking lot and spun around with Larissa in his arms. Then he bent and kissed this woman who'd given him more than he ever expected to have—love and a family.

Epilogue

Jake had decided that their honeymoon in Vegas had been too short and had surprised Larissa and Peter with a two-week trip through the Southeast following Jimmy Buffett's concert tour. This was their last night before heading back to Savannah. They were in Orlando in the parking lot at the TD Waterhouse Center. Jake and Peter wore identical unbuttoned Hawaiian-print shirts and khaki board shorts under grass skirts.

They were parked next to Courtney and Jen, two college girls they'd met at the concert in Miami the day before. They were grilling chicken and making margaritas. Jake came up behind Larissa and slipped his arms around her waist. He kissed her on the neck and whispered delicious promises in her ear.

Larissa leaned back against him and looked over at their son playing nearby. This was the life she'd been afraid to let herself dream of. But here it was nonetheless and it was so much more than she'd ever imagined.

"Mama, look," Peter said.

Their son proceeded to shake his hips and start singing fins. "Did Daddy teach you that?"

"Yes, come on, Daddy. Let's dance for her."

Peter and Jake did their hip-shaking dance for her and earned applause from the others in the parking lot. Larissa felt a sense of peace and belonging that she'd never thought to find. She closed her eyes. She realized that she was going to have to thank Jasmine Carmody for giving her the family she'd always dreamed of.

* * * * *

Watch for the next book in
DYNASTIES: THE DANFORTHS
when Brenda Jackson presents
SCANDAL BETWEEN THE SHEETS
in April.

Desire

**The captivating family saga of
the Danforths continues with**

SCANDAL BETWEEN
THE SHEETS
by
Brenda Jackson

(Silhouette Desire #1573)

There was one thing more seductive to hotshot reporter
Jasmine Carmody than a career-making story: tall, dark
businessman Wesley Brooks. But Wesley had his own
agenda, and would do whatever it took to ensure Jasmine
didn't uncover the scandal surrounding his close friends, the
Danforths…even if it meant getting closer still to Jasmine!

DYNASTIES: THE DANFORTHS

**A family of prominence…
tested by scandal, sustained by passion!**

Available April 2004 at your favorite retail outlet.

eHARLEQUIN.com

For **FREE online reading,** visit
www.eHarlequin.com now and enjoy:

Online Reads
Read **Daily** and **Weekly** chapters from
our Internet-exclusive stories by your
favorite authors.

Red-Hot Reads
Turn up the heat with one of our more
sensual online stories!

Interactive Novels
Cast your vote to help decide how these
stories unfold…then stay tuned!

Quick Reads
For shorter romantic reads, try our
collection of Poems, Toasts, & More!

Online Read Library
Miss one of our online reads?
Come here to catch up!

Reading Groups
Discuss, share and rave with other
community members!

For great reading online,
visit www.eHarlequin.com today!

INTONL

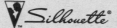

SPECIAL EDITION™

From *USA TODAY* bestselling author

SHERRYL WOODS

PRICELESS

(Silhouette Special Edition #1603)

Famed playboy Mick Carlton loved living
the fast life—with even faster women—
until he met Dr. Beth Browning.
Beth's reserved, quiet ways soon had him
wanting to believe in a slow and easy,
forever kind of love. Could Mack convince
Beth that his bachelor days were over?

**The second installment
in the popular miniseries**

**MILLION
DOLLAR
DESTINIES**

Three brothers discover all the riches money can't buy.

Available April 2004 at your favorite retail outlet.

COMING NEXT MONTH

#1573 SCANDAL BETWEEN THE SHEETS—Brenda Jackson
Dynasties: The Danforths
There was one thing more seductive to hotshot reporter Jasmine Carmody than a career-making story: tall, dark businessman Wesley Brooks. But Wesley had his own agenda, and would do whatever it took to ensure Jasmine didn't uncover the scandal surrounding his close friends, the Danforths...even if it meant getting *closer* still to Jasmine!

#1574 KEEPING BABY SECRET—Beverly Barton
The Protectors
The sexual chemistry had been explosive between Lurleen "Leenie" Patton and Frank Latimer. And their brief but passionate affair had resulted in a baby...a son Frank knew nothing about. When tragedy struck and their child was kidnapped, Leenie needed Frank to help find their son. But first she had to tell Frank he was a father....

#1575 A KEPT WOMAN—Sheri WhiteFeather
Mixing business and pleasure was against the rules for U.S. Marshal Zack Ryder. But Natalie Pascal—the very witness he was supposed to be protecting—tempted him beyond reason. The vulnerable vixen hid from a painful past, and Zack told himself he was only offering her comfort with his kisses, his touch....

#1576 FIT FOR A SHEIKH—Kristi Gold
Texas Cattleman's Club: The Stolen Baby
Sheikh Darin Shakir was on a mission to find and bring to justice a dangerous fugitive who used Las Vegas as his playground. But unforeseen circumstances had left Darin with bartending beauty Fiona Powers as his Sin City tour guide. Together, they were hot on the trail of the bad guy...and getting even hotter for each other!

#1577 SLOW DANCING WITH A TEXAN—Linda Conrad
Making time for men was never a concern for workaholic Lainie Gardner. That is, until a scary brush with a stalker forced her into hiding. Now, deep in the wilderness with her temporary bodyguard, Texas Ranger Sloan Abbot, the sexual tension sizzled. Could Lainie give in to her deepest desires for the headstrong cowboy?

#1578 A PASSIONATE PROPOSAL—Emilie Rose
Teacher Tracy Sullivan had had a crash on surgical resident Cort Lander *forever.* But when the sexy single dad hired *her* on as his baby's nanny, things got a little more heated. Tracy decided that getting over her crush meant giving in to passion...but would a no-strings-attached affair pave the way for a love beyond her wildest dreams?

SDCNM0304